Dolphin Boy Blue

Students and teachers lined the sides of the pool, screaming and cheering the boys on…As for Mickey, he couldn't hear the crowd; all he was aware of was the pounding of his heart and the rushing of the bubbles that swirled past his face. In the midst of this excitement, he began to hear the familiar clicks and squeaks that heralded Dana's approach. He couldn't believe that Dana was speaking to him while he was racing – it was like having his own personal coach urging him on.

Also from Collins

FELICE ARENA
DOLPHIN BOY BLUE

Collins
An imprint of HarperCollinsPublishers

First published in Great Britain by Collins in 1996
Collins is a imprint of HarperCollins*Publishers* Ltd.,
77 - 85 Fulham Palace Road, Hammersmith, London W6 8JB

1 3 5 7 9 8 6 4 2

ISBN 0 00 675198 9

The author asserts the moral right
to be identified as the author of the work

Printed and bound in Great Britain
by Caledonian International Book Manufacturing Ltd.,
Glasgow, G64

To my parents,
and to all those who share the same love as I do
for the ocean, swimming and of course...
dolphins.

CHAPTER ONE

In the small fishing village of Blue Rock, nothing much happens. It's a quiet town now with a population of about five thousand, but it used to be a major fishing port. Tourists drive through it on their way to more exciting places. Like most coastal towns, Blue Rock's busiest months are during the summer and even then the pace is slow compared to the rest of the world.

The biggest news to hit Blue Rock in its one hundred and fifty-two-year history was when it was voted the nation's Best Fish and Chip Town in 1973.

Apart from that, it's a pleasant place to park the family car, have an ice-cream, look across the bay and watch the sun set. That is until last year, when a boy called Mickey Nolan put Blue Rock on the map. But there was one other occasion when Blue Rock made the public eye. It was ten years ago, and Mickey was again part of the story. Unfortunately, he was involved in a tragedy that time...

Terrence Nolan was a strong, tall man, well-known in the Blue Rock community as a good man and a great fisherman. His grandfather had been a fisherman and so had his father, and Terrence – Terry to his mates – was carrying on the family tradition in an industry which was fast vanishing, especially in the bay and surrounding areas of Blue Rock. For Terry it was still a living; a way to support his family. But most of all, it was a job he loved.

His wife, Mary, worked part-time in the office of the local primary school, but most of her days were taken up with looking after their three-year-old son, Mickey.

Born and bred in Blue Rock, Mary had fallen in love with Terrence while she was still in High School, and today they were celebrating their fourth wedding anniversary. It was Mickey's birthday, too. The weather report on the radio had forecast a bright, sunny summer's day. It was just perfect for Terry and Mary to celebrate their anniversary with a boating trip in the bay.

Terry helped Mary and young Mickey board the *Bumper Joe*. It was Mickey's first time on his father's boat and he was eager to get going. The *Bumper Joe* was a fifteen-foot fishing vessel with a cabin, the kind of boat you could either stand up or sit down in to fish.

Once the boat was loaded, the Nolans headed out to sea. It seemed everyone else was taking advantage of the great weather too. A couple of jet skis were zipping about, twisting and turning through the blue water. Windsurfers were skimming over the waves and an adventurous tourist was having his first go at parasailing. A man skiing behind a speedboat waved frantically as he shot past the *Bumper Joe*. Mickey waved back. Terry slowly meandered the boat through the hub of marine activity. There were quite a few parties going on aboard the yachts, and the sounds of loud music, laughing, champagne glasses clinking and seagulls screeching, echoed across the water. Back on the beach, the distant crowd of people dotted along it looked like a large slice of fairy bread.

Terry decided to head further out, to escape the busy traffic. He steered the *Bumper Joe* towards the mouth of the bay; the gateway to the ocean. After a forty-minute journey, there was nothing else in sight except for a couple of seagulls that had followed them. Terry let down the anchor until it hit the seabed. On board, the Nolans opened the lavish picnic hamper Mary had made up that morning, and began their celebrations.

Mary and Terry toasted each other in champagne; they were both giggling as if they were teenagers again, on their first date. But Mickey was totally unaware of his parents' soppiness. He was half-way though his jam sandwich, when something caught his eye.

A long, dark shadow swam slowly past the bow of the boat.

'Mummy, Mummy, look, a big fish!' he cried.

By the time Mary and Terry got up to see what it was, the shadow had gone. Ten minutes later, away in the distance and about a hundred metres from the boat, Mickey saw the shadow under the water again.

'Mummy, look! That big fish is back again!'

This time, Mary caught a glimpse of a large grey fin submerging beneath the waves. Terrence was down below in the cabin, preoccupied with his fishing journal, and had missed the sighting again.

'What do you think it was?' he asked, coming up through the hatch when he heard Mickey's cries.

Mary wasn't sure. 'It looked like a shark, Terry! Why do you think it's circling the boat?'

'I really don't know.' Terry was mystified.

But Mickey was excited by the whole event. 'It was a happy fishie,' he said. 'It was smiling.'

Ignoring Mickey's comment, Terry decided to wait and watch for the so-called shark to reappear. They waited and waited. Twenty minutes passed.

'Well, whatever it was, it's gone now. And I think we'd better call it a day and head back in. Sorry, love, but I don't like the look of those clouds coming over.'

Mary followed Terry's gaze. In the distance, she could see the threatening dark skies of a storm creeping slowly towards them. For a moment, the eerie silence that accompanied its approach seemed over-whelming. As if they knew, the seagulls had disappeared. The temperature had dropped drastically. There was no doubt, the weather was changing rapidly – something that even the experienced Terry hadn't expected. The weather forecasts had predicted calm seas for the next three days, but it was clear that was not to be.

Now the sky was fully covered in a blanket of thunderous dark clouds. The sun had completely disappeared. A few moments earlier, the sea had been a calm, crystal blue, but now it was a cold, choppy, murky grey. The wind had picked up considerably and was whistling a ghost-like howl. The *Bumper Joe* was beginning to rock from side to side. Mary started packing up as fast as she could and she hauled the anchor up quickly. Terry was having problems starting the engine – there was no response as he repeatedly turned the ignition. He paused, then tried again. This time he could only get a groan, a cough and a splutter. It wouldn't kick over.

So as not to alarm Mickey, and trying to keep calm herself, Mary asked quietly, 'What's the problem?'

'It's the engine,' replied Terry, still turning the key.

'D'you think you can you fix it?'

'It sounds as if the problem's coming from the propellers down below. I'll have to go down and check it out.'

Mary was concerned now and she pleaded with Terry not to go in to the water. 'I can't let you swim down there, especially if there's a shark about!'

In the end, Terry decided to radio for help instead. 'Roy and some of the other lads are on their way,' said Terry, after he'd made contact.

'All we can do now is wait.' He tried to sound convincing, and reassured Mary that help would arrive before the storm hit. But they both knew, without saying a word to each other, that it would be a close-run thing.

The *Bumper Joe* was already riding some very large waves which were beginning to spew on to the deck. Terry could see swells of up to four metres or so only a short distance away. If help was coming, then it would have to be there fast – time was running out.

'Just hold on! We'll be OK!' said Terry, desperately trying to comfort Mary and Mickey.

Wearing life-jackets and sheltering in the cabin, they were all prepared for the worst. Mickey was clinging to his mother, trying hard to be brave and not cry.

Together, the furious rain and howling wind belted down on the feeble frame of the *Bumper Joe*.

Suddenly, without warning, the cabin window was smashed by the force of the beating waves. Mary screamed.

'Hold on!' yelled Terry.

Out of nowhere, as they clung to each other in horror, the dark curve of a gigantic and threatening wave came crashing down on them, swallowing up the *Bumper Joe*.

'Mummy!' screamed Mickey.

As if captured in a freeze frame, the next few moments were imprinted on Mickey's mind forever. What, in reality, lasted only seconds, seemed to go on for eternity. Mary tried desperately to keep a grip on her son, but the raging ocean separated both mother and child, wrenching them apart and tossing them about like two rags in a giant washing machine.

Mickey tried to call out, only to be forced to swallow huge mouthfuls of the cruel sea. Their arms stretched out to each other: Mary and Mickey were only a finger-tip distance apart, their eyes firmly fixed on one another. Mickey could see the terror in his mother's eyes. He could hear her scream out a helpless... 'I love you!... I love you!'

Now, Mickey could no longer see his mother. Then, like the after-shock of an earthquake, a second tidal wave came crashing on top of them, striking its final blow on the *Bumper Joe*. With that, the boat capsized.

Terry was the first to come up for air. He could see no sign of Mary or Mickey anywhere.

'Mickey! Mary!' Terry yelled, bobbing helplessly in the stormy waters, desperately seeking his family.

Mickey had already drifted away from the capsized boat. He wasn't conscious of what was happening to him. The dark blues and greens of the water, and the bright reflections of the bubbling, wind-whipped froth surrounded him and continued to push him further and further away from his mother and father and the wrecked boat.

Suddenly, Mickey began to hear what sounded to him like singing. It was beautiful. It was a female voice and was mixed with a series of piercing whistles that seemed to sing through his whole body.

In a state of numbed shock, Mickey wasn't sure whether he was dreaming or not. Wild ideas raced in and out of his young mind:

Mummy told me about angels, perhaps this is an angel singing to me, he thought. Mickey didn't feel scared any more. He listened to the voice.

'Sing away those broken tears
I am here for you
Swim away unwanted fears
I am here for you.'

It was repeated several times. From beneath the churning waves, a large shadow swam slowly up to Mickey, nudging him gently. Instinctively, Mickey grabbed hold of it. As he did so, he knew that this shadow, this mysterious singing sea angel, was there to help him...

CHAPTER TWO

In a couple of days, Mickey would be celebrating his thirteenth birthday. It would also be the week marking the tenth anniversary of their ill-fated boating accident – and his mother's death. During all these years, as if his memory had been erased in one fell swoop, Mickey had no recollection of the accident. Not one single memory remained. That was, until recently.

For the past two weeks, Mickey had been having recurring nightmares. He wasn't sure if they were imagined or if they were actual flashbacks of the accident. It didn't make sense to him that, after ten years, he was beginning to remember parts of it now. Most people had made an effort not to talk about the incident in front of him or his father, although at the time the event had been big news.

It had been well documented that Terry had been saved by the people he'd radioed for, but Mickey had been found lying on a beach, barely conscious. The fishermen who'd rescued Terry, and later picked up Mickey, say to this day that they'd witnessed a miracle. Through the roaring waves, they'd seen Mickey carried to the safety of the beach by a large, bottle-nosed dolphin.

The story of the dolphin rescue had not only made the local news, but had attracted national coverage. The media from all over the country had arrived in the small town of Blue Rock to report on it. The Best Fish and Chip Town's name was on everyone's lips. Well, at least for a week. Then the story died as quickly as it had come, and it was soon yesterday's news. Blue Rock was once again just another town where nothing much happened. But for Mickey and Terry, it was something they'd have to live with for the rest of their lives.

'No! No! No!' screamed Mickey.

It was the middle of the night and once again Mickey was having a nightmare.

Awoken by the scream, Terry rushed to his son's bedside. He switched on Mickey's light and saw him sitting upright in bed, a cold sweat pouring off him as he panted with fright.

'Son, are you all right?' Terry asked, very concerned.

'Dad, what's happening? It felt so real.' Mickey was still breathing heavily. On the other occasions he'd had nightmares, he'd said he was OK and had turned over and gone back to sleep. But this time, Terry made him talk about it.

'I— I could see Mum's face, and she had her arms stretched out to me, wanting me to come to her. But we were both underwater. As I swam closer to her, she was being sucked away from me, and no matter how many times I tried to get near her, we just couldn't grab hold of each other!'

Terry didn't know what to say. So many times he too had experienced similar dreams. But they'd become less frequent as time went by.

'Son, I have no idea why you're having these sort of dreams now. But maybe it's Mum's way of saying she's still around.'

'Do you really believe that, Dad? I mean, if she's in heaven, do you think she's looking down at us now?' Mickey asked, softly.

Terry paused. It had been some time since he and Mickey had talked intimately about anything, especially Mary's death. And he didn't find it easy to express his emotions. In all the years Mickey could remember, he had never once seen his father cry.

'Mick... Not a day goes by when I don't think of your mother... And maybe she can see us, who knows? All I do know is that I will never, ever forget her. She will always be a part of me... of us.'

For a moment, nothing else was said between them. Mickey really wanted to hug his father, but somehow he couldn't. Terry was thinking the same thing, but instead he quickly changed the subject.

'If you're feeling OK now, I think we should try getting back to sleep. I don't want those fish getting away, just because I'm tired!'

Minutes later, the lights were off and Mickey was once again tucked up in bed. He heard his father shut his bedroom door but, in the still darkness, Mickey found it difficult to take his advice and go back to sleep. His mind was working overtime. So many times he'd wondered what his mother would be like if she were still alive. Now he couldn't stop thinking about the dream.

He switched on his bedside lamp and from underneath his bed slid out a scrapbook. He flicked slowly through it. It was a very special scrapbook where he kept photos of his mother. Amongst the photos, there were also some press cuttings.

BOY SAVED BY DOLPHIN, TRAGEDY ENDS IN MIRACLE

and

DOLPHIN BOY'S BEST FRIEND

Mickey had lost count of how many times he'd read them, but he always referred to his scrapbook whenever he was missing his mum – so now seemed the right moment.

As morning arrived, Mickey did get back to sleep. He woke late to find the scrapbook spread out across his face. It was Sunday and the distant chime of church bells was ringing through the streets of Blue Rock. Terry had been up for hours already, and was still out in the bay, fishing. He wouldn't be home until lunch time.

Once showered and dressed, Mickey went about his usual household chores. Because his father was busy at work, he had learnt to fend for himself, especially in the last couple of years, although Terry still did most of the cooking. With the final bit of vacuuming done, Mickey decided to go down to meet his father at the docks. Maybe today would be the day he could convince him to take him out on the boat. Ever since the accident, Terry had never got over his wife's death at sea, in *his* boat. And bearing that guilt, he had forbidden Mickey to go out on *any* boat, either with him or with any of the other fishermen.

But Mickey felt deprived. Not only did he long for a boat trip but he was curious to see where the accident had happened, especially now, with the dreams he'd been having. But there was more to it than that. It was something Mickey couldn't quite explain himself. His urge to go out into the middle of the ocean grew stronger and stronger each day. But no matter how many times Mickey pleaded with his father, the answer was always a definite no!

It took Mickey a good twenty minutes to walk from his house to the docks, even though it was downhill all the way. There were two levels to Blue Rock – the top half and the bottom half. It was built along the cliffs, with one main shopping street that zig-zagged its way through the middle of town from top to bottom; beginning down at the beach-front coastal road, and then carving its way up to Butler's Lighthouse, the highest point of the small sea resort.

Mickey lived in the top half. From their kitchen window he could see over most of Blue Rock, right down to the ocean. Only a couple of blocks away were his school, Blue Rock High, and the local swimming pool.

As he approached the pier, Mickey could

see that his father's boat hadn't yet arrived amongst the fleet of fishing vessels. Passing by, he couldn't help overhear some tourists talking enthusiastically about their visit to the town.

'Oh, this coastline! What a magnificent sight!' and they clicked away with their expensive cameras which dangled from their necks. Mickey looked back up towards the town. Being a local, he sometimes took it for granted and forgot how beautiful Blue Rock really was.

Wedged between awesome, towering limestone cliffs, the sheer beauty of its surrounding rugged coastline made the perfect backdrop. Throughout the day, especially on long, sunny summer days, the colour of the limestone would change. At dawn, when the sun was just rising, the light was neither day or night, and the cliffs mirrored the still morning ocean reflecting a washed pale blue. It was because of this that the town had been called Blue Rock.

In the middle of the day, the colours would vary from bright sandy cream to dusty brown.

But it was in the late afternoon, at dusk, when the cliff face really came alive. In a span of only minutes, the surface of the rock changed from striking golden tones of yellow, orange and mustard to vibrant splashes of rich pinks and rusty reds. It was a natural phenomenon that the locals, including Mickey, couldn't help but be proud of.

Mickey smiled at the tourists and went on his way, happily. The pier was crowded with locals and visitors together. It had a market-like atmosphere and was always busy on the weekends. People would buy their fish fresh, directly from the boats. Fishermen would sell some of the leftovers from their catch, doing their very best to outbid each other.

'Get your snapper here! The best snapper you'll ever taste! Get your snapper here!' one was shouting now.

'Forget the snapper! What you want is a succulent piece of hake! Get your hake here!' yelled another.

Mickey pushed his way through the jostling crowd. Most of the boats were docked against one side of the pier. Terry usually kept his at the very end. Mickey headed in that direction and decided to wait for his father there.

Not looking where he was going, Mickey bumped straight into a woman carrying a basket of fish. She dropped it on the ground.

'I'm sorry,' apologized Mickey. Quickly he crouched down to help the lady pick up her fish.

'That's all right, dear. It's not for me, it's for my cats,' she said.

Mickey looked up and saw that the woman was smiling at him. In fact, she couldn't stop smiling at him. Mickey apologized again but she didn't say a thing, she just kept staring at him.

'Um... I think I'd better get going,' said Mickey, beginning to feel uncomfortable. The lady looked interesting, but slightly odd, with huge silver earrings and a silk scarf around her shoulders. She must have been very beautiful when she was young, thought Mickey.

But still she didn't say a word, she just nodded, still grinning, as Mickey walked off. He'd ambled a short distance before he looked back over his shoulder and saw the lady was still standing in the same spot, staring after him.

Boy! She's weird, thought Mickey. A few seconds later, he took another look back. Standing on the tips of his toes, Mickey peered through the crowd and saw that the lady had gone. It was as if she'd disappeared into thin air.

'Hey kid! Throw me that bucket, will ya?'

Mickey turned and saw that a man in a boat was talking to him. Mickey threw the bucket over. He knew all the fishermen in the area, but this guy was new to him. The man introduced himself to Mickey and told him that he'd just moved to Blue Rock. Mickey asked him if knew his father and if so had he seen him make his way in from the bay. The new fisherman said he knew Terry, but hadn't seen him that morning.

Mickey waited for a while, staring out to sea, but there was still no sign of his father. Just as he was about to walk home, the fisherman yelled out to Mickey.

'Hey, kid! I'm about to head out again. You can come with me, if you want. We might see your dad out there.'

Mickey stopped dead in his tracks. That's right, he thought. Unlike the other fishermen, this guy doesn't know about my father's ban! Mickey looked around. This seemed like a perfect opportunity: his father's workmates were busy selling fish – no-one would see him go. It was an offer he couldn't refuse – the temptation was too great.

He turned back to the fisherman. 'All right, that would be great... Thanks, mister!' he said, excitedly.

Once in the boat, Mickey's heart began to pound. He couldn't believe that he was finally going out to sea.

'Here, put this on,' said the fisherman, throwing Mickey a lifejacket. As he was slipping it over his head, someone started yelling at him from the pier.

'What the heck do you think you're doing, young man?'

It was Terry! Mickey jumped, surprised and guilty at being caught out. Terry had anchored his boat a few metres away from shore and had come in with another fisherman. Mickey stammered a feeble excuse.

'Um... I... was coming to find you, Dad... I was worried... yeah, that's it... I was worried about you,' he finished, lamely.

'Don't give me that! Get out of that boat. NOW!' shouted Terry, angrily.

The new fisherman couldn't understand what was going on.

'Sorry, Bill,' said Terry. 'It's not your fault, I'll explain everything later.'

Mickey hopped out of the boat and climbed his way up the pier.

Terry grabbed him by the arm and, trying to keep his voice down so as not to cause a scene, said, 'How many times do I have to tell you? You're not allowed to go out on *any* boat!'

Mickey tried to defend himself. 'Well, it's a stupid rule, Dad! It's not fair! I think I'm old enough to do what I want!' he shouted.

'Not while you're living under my roof, young man! I'm very disappointed in you, Mick... Now get on home!' Terry's voice had risen. It was clear they were both very upset. Mickey tried hard not to sob. The argument had attracted a couple of curious onlookers and even some of the fishermen looked over to see what all the fuss was about.

'We'll talk about this when I get home,' said Terry, embarrassed.

Mickey didn't answer. He walked away sulkily and for the rest of the day, he wandered about the streets of Blue Rock, finally ending up at the cemetery.

Sitting by his mother's grave, where he often came, he began to tell her about his day.

'Mum, please make tomorrow a better day than today. I'm thirteen tomorrow and...' he stopped. The caretaker of the cemetery had seen him talking to himself. Mickey stood up, feeling silly, even though he often found himself talking to his mother like this, but very soon the man carried on about his own business.

Mickey leant forward and whispered, 'I'm sorry I upset Dad and I hope things'll be better tomorrow. I'll see you later, Mum.'

As he made his way out of the cemetery and headed home, he didn't know that something special was about to happen –

something that was going to make tomorrow, his thirteenth birthday, very different from all the others.

CHAPTER THREE

Mickey had a friend, someone he could talk to about almost anything, no matter how silly or personal it was. She could understand him better than anyone else. Her name was Jo. Joanne Powell – everyone called her Jo – was Mickey's next-door neighbour. The Powells had been like a second family to Mickey, and Jo and he had grown up together. Whenever Terry went out on longer fishing trips than usual, Mickey would stay with the Powells. Like Mickey, Jo was an only child, and Mr and Mrs Powell adored having him around. Jo and Mickey did everything together – they went to the movies, watched TV, went swimming together and sat in class next to each other.

Now, they were both in the school yard having lunch.

'This is so cool!' Mickey was raving about the present Jo had given him. It was a pendant on a black leather thong, shaped like a dolphin and carved from a stone.

'What stone did you say it was again? And where did you get it?' Mickey was delighted and so was Jo. There was nothing more she wanted than to make Mickey happy.

'It's turquoise and I got it from that store called Madam Karma's, in Allen Street. I saw it on display in the window. I'm not sure if the lady who served me was Madam Karma or not, but if she was, she is nothing like the kids at school say she is. She turned out to be really nice. She knew heaps of information about dolphins, too!'

Jo had Mickey's full attention now. She knew that he'd always had a fascination with dolphins, especially because his life had been saved by one. As Jo helped tie the pendant around Mickey's neck, she told him what she'd learnt from the woman in the craft shop.

'Did you know that a dolphin has a bigger

brain than humans, and that there are one hundred and thirty-two known species? And did you know that the largest dolphin of them all is the Killer Whale? And get this... Did you know that apart from humans, dolphins are the only creatures on earth who cry tears?'

Mickey wasn't that surprised at what Jo was telling him. He'd always felt that dolphins were amazing creatures. Now he really wanted to visit this Madam Karma's store. He still couldn't get over his beautiful present. He really loved it.

'Wow, this is so cool, Jo!' he said again.

'You've already said that, you dummy!' Jo looked thrilled, too.

'Well, it is! It's the best present I'll get this year. Thanks again, mate!' Mickey leant over and gave Jo a brotherly kiss on the cheek. She blushed. Just then, the school bell sounded.

'Do you still wanna go swimming this afternoon?' said Mickey.

'You bet,' Jo said, eagerly.

'OK. See you in front of the school, straight after last period.' Mickey ran off to class. It was the only time during their week's timetable that

Jo and Mickey had separate classes. Double art for Mickey and double science for Jo.

Later, as Mickey waited for Jo underneath the Blue Rock High School sign, a group of girls headed his way. Not just any group of girls – these girls were the prettiest and most popular in Mickey's year, and leading the group was Dominique Peterson. The boys in Mickey's class referred to her as 'the ultimate babe', but Jo had always thought she was 'the ultimate bimbo' and was seriously upset when Mickey spoke about her.

'She doesn't even know you exist!'

'Yes she does! How do you know, anyway?' Mickey would say in defence.

'Because someone like Dominique Peterson doesn't care about anyone but herself. She's got such a big ego that if you're not in the "in-crowd", you're not worth anything to her.'

Jo was being honest, and truthful. Dominique really wasn't a nice person but the boys, Mickey included, thought she looked gorgeous. She had long, shiny blonde hair that bounced from side to side when she walked. (Secretly, Mickey thought she looked like the girl in a shampoo commercial!)

Right at that moment, Dominique was heading straight towards him.

Wow, she's actually coming over to speak to me, thought Mickey. She'll come over and say 'I think you're cute' and then I'll stare into her blue eyes and— Mickey's imagination was getting out of hand.

Now he tried desperately to say hello, but found himself spluttering and stuttering, and finally managed a feeble, high-pitched 'Hi, ya!'

'Get out of my way, you jerk!' Dominique snapped, taking some gum out of her mouth and throwing it into the rubbish bin Mickey was standing next to. Then she and her gang ran giggling away.

As Mickey stood there blushing, Jo ran over; she'd witnessed the whole scene. She put her hand on Mickey's back. 'So how about that swim, mate?'

Even though Mickey's ego was deflated, he wasn't going to let a little incident like that ruin his birthday. He still had half a day left, and he wanted nothing more than to do what he loved best – swimming!

Once at the beach, Mickey and Jo set off along the water's edge, past the main tourist area, over some rocks and then around to the next cove where the beach wasn't usually so busy.

It was a pretty, secluded little cove, where the smooth white sand only attracted a few tourists, the occasional nude bather and some keen body surfers. The waves were too small for board surfers, unless they were beginners, but they were just perfect for swimmers who were strong enough to propel themselves along with the breakers.

Before Jo could even get her school shoes off, Mickey was in the water. He was a fantastic swimmer and always showed off in front of Jo, diving and springing buoyantly out of the crashing surf.

Mickey loved being in the water, though many people had thought, after the accident, that he would have been too frightened to go near the sea. But instead, he was drawn to it, and by the time he was six years old, he was a strong swimmer. For as long as Jo could remember, Mickey had swum every day of the summer holidays. She once asked him why he loved swimming so much:

'I don't know. It's another world in the sea and every time I swim, I feel great!' And that was his answer – no other reason except that it made him feel good.

'Hey, Mickey, it's time to go. Your dad's probably wondering where we are. Mickey!'

He couldn't hear Jo. As always, he'd chosen to swim underneath the breaking waves, beneath the surface where it teemed with marine life. Mickey loved it. At first his eyes would sting from the salt water, but as soon as they'd adjusted, his view of the colourful world below was as clear as the crystal blue water itself. Mickey could feel the sun's warm rays beating against his back. The rays reflected down through the water, making the coral and the schools of tiny silver fish that frequently swam in the area glisten and sparkle. The golden sand of the seabed swayed in time to the crashing surf above. Mickey once saw a stingray glide majestically only inches above the seabed. He'd followed it as long as he'd been physically able.

Sometimes, without noticing it, Mickey would leave the safety of the warm, clear, shallow water and venture further out to the colder, darker and deeper ocean that lay ahead of him. Although it frightened Jo when he swam out so far, Mickey loved it. He would float in the water and stare at the mass of blue, wondering about his mother, only then realizing that it was time to surface for air.

'Mickey!' Jo was still shouting for him. 'Have you forgotten? Your dad's cooking you a birthday dinner!'

'Oh yeah,' Mickey had surfaced and was carving his way through the waves towards her.

Once he was back on the beach, they quickly grabbed their belongings and scampered off home.

'...happy birthday, dear Mickey. Happy birthday to you,' sang Jo and Terry.

The usual birthday ritual followed. Mickey blew out his candles, made a wish and then cut the cake. Terry left the room to get Mickey's present.

'So what do you think he's got you?' asked Jo.

Mickey said he didn't care – the best present he could receive from his father would be if he allowed him to go out on a boat. But he knew he wasn't going to get that this evening.

Terry watched proudly as Mickey ripped open his present. It was a book called *The Book of 101 Puzzles and Conundrums*. Mickey tried to pretend that he liked it, but it was no use – Terry could see the disappointment on his son's face. He tried to cover the awkward moment by making conversation with Jo.

'Now make sure, Jo, that you don't forget to take a couple of slices of birthday cake for your parents.'

Jo felt sorry for both of them. 'Thanks, Mr Nolan, I will. In fact I'd better head off. Thanks again for the lovely meal. See ya, Mick!' she called as she went.

Mickey and Terry were in the kitchen doing the washing-up when Terry confronted Mickey about his present. 'I'm sorry you don't like it, Mickey. I wasn't really sure what you wanted,' he said.

Mickey tried to convince his father that the present was OK but Terry didn't believe him.

'If it's something specific you want, maybe I can still get it for you. What did you really want?'

'Well...' said Mickey, tentatively. 'The birthday present I really wanted was... Look it doesn't matter, Dad!'

But Terry was still pushing. 'No, no. You've started now, what *did* you want?'

Mickey stopped washing the dishes. He looked at his father and took a deep breath. 'The present I really wanted was... you to let me go out on a boat!'

Terry went very silent. All he did was shake his head. 'So that's what this was all about. You're pushing it, son. Enough's enough! Don't spoil your birthday.'

And before long, they were at it again, arguing as they had on the pier. In the end, they went to bed, upset with each other.

Later that night, Mickey found it difficult to get to sleep. He was still feeling angry at his father. So much so, he decided to sneak out of the house, there and then.

'I'll show him!' he said emotionally to himself. 'I'll take the boat out myself!'

Outside, he crouched down and crawled quietly past his dad's bedroom window, then crept across the front lawn, finally making a dash past Jo's house. Mickey ran as fast as possible, with tears streaming down his face from the salty night air blowing into his eyes – or maybe because he was really crying. All he knew was that his father wasn't going to stop him this time!

CHAPTER FOUR

Mickey didn't stop running until he reached the beach front. Once there, he suddenly came to his senses. He realized that he was acting in haste, and no matter how much he disagreed with his father, he didn't want to hurt him. It would be pure foolishness to take the boat out by himself. He didn't even know how to drive it!

He looked around him at the town of Blue Rock, fast asleep – he had never seen it like that before. As he glanced down at his watch, he saw it was almost one o'clock in the morning. The still streets made Mickey feel as if he was the only person in the world. All he could hear was a dog barking in the distance and the surf crashing on to the beach. Not wanting to go back home right away, Mickey decided to walk to the cove where he and Jo had swum earlier that afternoon.

He took off his shoes and socks, rolled up his jeans and splashed along the edge of the water. The baby waves rolled rhythmically, all white and frothy like a bubble bath, greeting Mickey's feet. Surprisingly, the water wasn't cold. It was a mild night, with just an occasional, refreshing salt breeze spraying up from the calm ocean. In the sky was a full, golden moon, hanging loosely above the horizon, casting its delicate night light upon the snoozing coastal town below. Mickey stared at it in wonder. It was breathtaking. He could see for miles over the water. Catching the moonlight, the ocean looked as if it was blanketed with sparkling diamonds, twinkling as bright as the stars above. Mickey couldn't believe what everyone missed while they slept. It was way better than any Christmas decorations he'd ever seen.

When he reached the cove, Mickey sprawled on the sand and, lying on his back, he looked directly up at the brilliant constellations above him. He was searching for the Southern Cross. There it is! he said to himself, feeling reassured that it was still up there. He saw the Milky Way and felt like an ant in comparison, as he stared at the sheer vastness of the midnight sky like a dome over his head. When he focused on the stars, Mickey began to feel very tired. He found himself drifting slowly into a heavy sleep. As he did so, strange sounds seemed to be whirling around inside his head. They were like eerie clicks and squeaks, fading in and out, coming close to him and then, just as quickly, drifting away.

Mickey thought he had been dreaming; in fact, he was almost fully asleep. That was until he began to hear someone singing. Suddenly, he stood up, his heart beginning to thump.

'Who's there?' yelled Mickey in the deepest voice he could muster – he didn't want to appear scared.

He looked behind him and saw only the moonlit cliff face looming down on him. But he felt a strong presence; he could feel someone or something was watching him.

After a few minutes of keeping completely still, Mickey began to wonder whether it had been a dream and he started to make his way back home. But he'd only gone a few steps when it happpened again! Someone was singing! Mickey froze. Whoever it was seemed to be standing directly behind him. He slowly turned round, inch by inch, holding his breath... Nothing! What was going on? He could still hear the singing. It definitely sounded like a female voice. But it was unusual; nothing like he had ever heard anywhere before. Mickey looked frantically around, but still he could see no-one. He began to think the voice sounded as if it was coming from beneath the water. The haunting aria was still ringing in his ears – it wasn't deafening but it sent a tingling sensation through his whole body.

Suddenly, Mickey wasn't feeling scared any more. 'If this is a joke, I'm not laughing... You can come out whoever you are!' he said, bravely.

But the voice continued to sing. Mickey

couldn't help feeling something extra-ordinary was happening. For some reason, the angelic voice he was hearing sounded familiar. He felt compelled to listen. At first it had sounded like a combination of clicks, squeaks and high-pitched whistles, but when Mickey focused on them and concentrated hard, he could hear lyrical words within them. The voice was singing...

> *'Look to my world, you'll hear my song*
> *Just believe, it won't take long*
> *Under blue, beneath its face*
> *There I swim, my home, my place.'*

Mickey worked out from the song that it was definitely beneath the ocean, whoever or whatever it was. 'What are you?' he asked.

There was a chorus of whistles and, as Mickey listened, he couldn't believe what he was hearing. He concentrated again, making sure that his first interpretation was correct.

'You're a dolphin – swimming in the bay!' said Mickey, stunned. He couldn't believe it! This strange encounter was getting more weird by the minute. The dolphin went on, telling him her name was Dananihplod, or Dana as she was known.

How is this possible? How can we hear each other? thought Mickey.

In a harmony of low, registered clicks, Dana began to answer Mickey's thoughts.

Surprised because he hadn't even opened his mouth, Mickey interrupted Dana's next song. 'Hold on! Hold on!' he cried, confused. 'How did you know what I was thinking?' Again, he had to be patient and listen to her lyrics.

> *'When, like a waking sleep, and no other thing*
> *Your mind is best to hear me sing*
> *Imagine us, and you will find*
> *When need to speak, speak mind to mind.'*

It took Mickey a few moments to decipher what Dana was saying. Then it dawned on him – and he decided to test out what he was thinking.

Dana? Can you hear me? thought Mickey.

Suddenly, swirling squeaks rushed back into his head. Dana repeated the song and then ended by saying... yes! That confirmed it – as much as Mickey found it difficult to believe – he was truly talking to a dolphin, telepathically!

Mickey had to sit down for a few seconds to contemplate this revelation. He had to stop and pinch himself. Who would believe him? he thought. As he and Dana talked, Mickey soon realized that whenever Dana spoke, she did so in song. Even the most simple answers like 'yes' and 'no' were answered in a kind of music. Sometimes Mickey had to ask Dana to repeat a song because, as beautiful and poetic as they were, they were very complex. The more they spoke, the better Mickey's interpretation of Dana's clicks and whistles became. It was as if they were two long-lost friends. Dana did most of the talking and Mickey was content just to lie on the sand and take everything in. Listening to Dana's voice made him feel fantastic.

Mickey did have one important question he was dying to ask, but felt hesitant. Perhaps

Dana would not be able to confirm his suspicions? Mickey decided to leave it for the time being and ask her something else.

'You said that more dolphins and whales are making themselves known to man. What do you mean?'

Dana repeated her song:

'*We sing our songs to show we care*
Though seasons pass, we're always there
Moon to moon, not long will it be
For man and dolphin to be together and
free.

'*Whales rejoice at what soon will be*
known
When you, the man, is fully grown
Then we will all have work to do
And speak our songs, like me to you.'

Wow! thought Mickey. I think I understand. You're saying that dolphins and whales have been around for centuries and sometime in the future people will be able to speak to them. That's so cool! he thought.

Momentarily, he forgot that that's what he was already doing.

'Dana, am I the first person dolphins have decided to speak to?' he asked in a small voice.

'It may feel that you are the only one
But songs to others have long begun.'

Mickey's ego was a little deflated but he understood that dolphins were admired by people all over the world, so he carried on listening.

'You are the first, for me, my one
Each to our own, our chosen one.'

'Why me?' interrupted Mickey.

'Amongst the love, I hear your pain
Inside your heart, you cry like rain.
Infant, child, not yet a man
You grow this time as quick as you can.'

Mickey was a little confused. Was it possible that she could hear his thoughts *and* sense how he felt, too? he couldn't help wondering.

There was more to the song...

'For us to help one, we help all
Together we join, a unified call
The planet is ill, please heed what we say
It is for us to teach and show you the way.
To stop man spilling blood, we plea
Or creatures all will no longer be
Dolphins and whales, our motto we sing
Love and freedom to everything.'

There was silence between them. Mickey could sense the sadness in her song. He said nothing but Dana noticed that Mickey was tired and his concentration was fading. As Mickey fell asleep, Dana sang him a tune she called The Lullaby Song.

'Listen to the surf dance to and fro
In your dream you will go
Safe and warm in shallow blue
Feel the sun's touch shine on you
But when you sleep, all night long
You're sure to hear this lullaby song.'

Mickey slept for hours on the soft sand. It wasn't until he heard the loud squawking of seagulls, that he woke to see it was sunrise.

'Oh no! It's morning already!' Mickey said to himself, desperately trying to get his shoes and socks on as quickly as possible. His watch read six o'clock. He knew that was the time his father would be awake and having breakfast. Now he'd have to be extremely careful trying to slip back into the house without being caught. He just hoped that his father wouldn't check his bedroom. Normally, he didn't – he was always rushing to get to his boat. In his haste, Mickey almost forgot about Dana. Now he looked out to sea, and thought as hard as he could.

'Dana?' he asked.

There was no response – but Mickey sensed she was still out there. Now there was no time to waste – he had to get back. He would come back and see Dana again, after school.

Turning into his street and running as fast as he could, Mickey saw a car heading towards him. As it drew closer, he could see it was his father! He had to think quickly. Like a goalkeeper fully stretched to make his save, Mickey dived behind some garbage bins on the side of the road.

Just then, his father drove by, but he didn't see him.

'Phew!' sighed Mickey, relieved. The coast was clear. Back at his house, he climbed in through his bedroom window – he'd made it. Mickey was home at last!

CHAPTER FIVE

'Wake up, Mickey, wake up!' Jo was nudging him.

They were sitting next to each other in their final period at school. Mickey had been tired all day; talking to Dana for most of the night had really taken it out of him. He hadn't told Jo what had happened, but she knew something was up.

'What?' Mickey woke up with a start and found his history teacher standing over him. 'Can you repeat the question, sir?' he asked nervously.

'No! I will not repeat the question, but I expect you to have the courtesy to stay awake next time you come into my class.'

'Yes, sir, I will.' Mickey felt terrible, but it looked as if he was going to be spared extra homework – the bell rang just at that moment.

'Class dismissed. See you tomorrow. Oh, and Mickey, please get some sleep tonight!'

As the students shuffled out of the classroom, Jo grabbed Mickey. 'What's wrong?' she asked. 'You've been acting weird all day.'

Mickey was hesitant about telling anyone about his magical encounter. He knew that the previous night was incredible, and he realized it was very special. Something this special was best kept to himself, he thought. But he was dying to tell someone about it. Someone he knew he could also trust and Jo was the most likely person.

'Look, I'll explain everything when we go swimming,' he said.

And so he did. Jo wasn't sure how to react to the news. It did cross her mind that Mickey had flipped his lid, but Mickey tried to convince her that he really wasn't crazy.

'Jo, I know it's hard to believe – I didn't believe it myself at first. But when Dana sang to me—'

'She *sings*?' Jo couldn't help giggling.

Surprised and annoyed by her reaction, Mickey said, 'Yes! She sings! She speaks to me through her songs. The same way that dolphins and whales communicate with each other.'

Jo sensed that she'd upset Mickey and she stopped giggling.

'Out of everyone, I thought you'd be the one who'd believe me,' he said, sadly.

Jo felt terrible. But she felt touched that Mickey had turned to her before anyone else. 'I'm sorry, Mickey. It's just a bit difficult to understand exactly what you're telling me.' Jo took his hand affectionately and said, 'Mick... I believe you... If *you* say it happened, then I believe you!' and they both smiled.

After an hour's swimming, Mickey tried to communicate with Dana again. His initial plan was to ask her to come and greet him and Jo at the beach. After spending a whole night talking to each other, it was only natural that Mickey wanted to see her for real, even though she had mentioned to him that she swam miles out in the ocean.

As the late afternoon set in, it was clear that Mickey was getting more upset and frustrated. It got to the point where Mickey, swimming under the waves, tried to imitate Dana's clicks and squeaks himself. He even tried to swim like her – kicking his legs together in the same motion that a dolphin might use to move its tail. But it was no use, he couldn't hear a single song. Why didn't Dana answer his thoughts?

When Jo yelled to him that they ought to go, Mickey was reluctant to leave.

'Jo, she's out there! She is!' he insisted.

On the way home, both of them were silent. Jo thought it best to keep quiet. Mickey was beginning to question himself now. Maybe it *had* all been a dream? Perhaps he was going crazy? But he found it hard not to believe in Dana. I did, I did speak to her, he said to himself.

There was only one thing Mickey felt he could do – go out on a boat and find Dana. And that would mean talking to his father again!

'Please, Dad? Forget all the other excuses, this is for real... You've got to believe me!'

'Look, Mick, you leave the house in the middle of the night and you expect me to believe this rubbish?'

'But Dad, it did happen! You *have* to believe me – for Mum's sake!'

'Why don't you understand, Mickey, your mother's never coming back!' Terry sounded upset and angry.

'But you don't, do you, Dad?' Mickey answered.

And his son had hit a sore point. It was true, Terry still found it difficult not having his wife beside him. He didn't answer. He just walked out of the room, leaving Mickey feeling terrible. He hated having arguments with his dad. He really loved him and this was always the only subject they fought over. But this time he wasn't going to give up – he knew that Dana really *was* swimming out in the bay.

That night, before going to sleep, Mickey set his alarm for midnight. He was determined to sneak out of the house again. Stretched out in bed, it wasn't long before Mickey began drifting off to sleep. To his surprise, he thought he could hear Dana's singing. It was very faint to begin with but, as he focused his mind on it, the song grew louder and louder until it was clearly ringing in his head.

I'm in my room, nowhere near the beach. How could this be happening? thought Mickey. 'Dana, is that you?' he said into the darkness. Dana told him it was. Mickey was thrilled, and also relieved. Just for a moment, he had been having doubts himself.

Glad that last night's happenings were not over, he asked Dana how it was that he could speak to her from his own bedroom, nowhere near the sea.

She answered once again, in the voice that Mickey had been yearning to hear all day.

'Where you are, you will find
Body is far, but closer is mind
Whether on land or in the sea
Believe in yourself and picture me.'

Mickey spoke his thoughts. 'But Dana, I did picture you, but you didn't answer. Will I ever see you?'

'As waters cool by the season
So I act for a reason.'

'What reason?' asked Mickey, curious now
and determined to find an answer.

'To help you, is one thing
But your father needs to sing
He is sad, much like you
So I'm here for him, too.'

'My dad? You're telling me the reason you
couldn't come on to the beach is because my
father needs help?' What could Dana mean?

'For us to meet, there's only one way
You come to me, out far away.'

Mickey panicked. 'But Dana! I can't come
out to you. My father won't let me on the boat
– you know that, I told you last night.'
Dana sang in response.

'Be patient, Mickey, time is the key
Where changes will come, just wait and see

You and your father, together you'll grow
You'll come and meet me, that I know.'

Mickey, was confused, but he said sorry to Dana for showing his frustration. They began to talk and talk, and from then on they talked every night.

Every evening, Dana ended their communcations by singing Mickey to sleep with the Lullaby Song. Mickey talked about his days at school, and Dana sang about her life experiences. She once told him about the time she was almost killed.

'The chase was on for us to feed
Amongst the pod, I was to lead
Thirty of us worked as one
To catch the fish was always fun
The men of evil did their thing
They trapped us all in a wall of string
No way out, my brother cried
Couldn't escape even though we tried
My family all dying, and so was I
Couldn't give up, still had to try
In one gulp, I made my bet

*To dive below and rush the net
And there it was, I could see
An opening so big, I could be free
But calling back to the deathly fate
No one followed, it was much too late.'*

Mickey found himself in tears after listening to Dana's tragic story. He felt guilty that she had lost her entire family because of Man. Now he could understand why Dana felt the same pain as he did.

A couple of weeks went by before Mickey plucked up enough courage to ask the question he had kept inside himself all this time. Dana could sense his nervousness. Mickey decided to communicate his thoughts very quickly.

'When I was a boy, were you the one who saved me?' There, he'd said it.

There was a pause. Dana let out a series of very high-pitched whistles – nothing like she had sung to Mickey in the past two weeks. But for some strange reason, this song triggered something in Mickey's memory.

Suddenly, he saw flashbacks of his accident – the same ones he'd had in his dreams, which had stopped since he'd met Dana. He could see himself reaching out to his mother, and then she was gone.

But someone or something else was there with him. He could sense whatever it was, looking at him. He focused hard and could see that he was staring right into the eye of a dolphin! Could it be he was remembering Dana? The more the flashback continued, the more Mickey was remembering. Out of nowhere, he sensed that the high-pitched whistles that Dana was singing to him were familiar.

'It *was* you! You're the dolphin who saved me!' yelled Mickey, excitedly. 'I know it was you, I can remember the words you sang.' Then Mickey and Dana sang together.

'Sing *away those broken tears*
I am here for you
Swim away unwanted fears
I am here for you.'

Together they repeated the chorus over and over again. Mickey was quite overcome. It was the answer he'd always wanted to hear. But Dana sensed he wanted to ask her something else. And Mickey did have another question for her, something more serious to do with the accident. But he decided not to ask – not just yet anyway. Instead, he was over the moon that he'd been reunited with the dolphin who'd saved his life!

CHAPTER SIX

The following day, Blue Rock High was having its annual Swimming Sports Gala. For sports days – athletics or any other sport – students were randomly separated into four house teams: Red, Green, Blue and Gold. The team which had the most points at the end of the competition would win.

Today Mickey was put into Blue House and Jo was representing the Reds. As they were the juniors of the school, it would be the first time they had taken part in the swimming gala. At their primary school there had never been such competitions, so this was very exciting for them both – especially Jo, who was practically bursting with anticipation.

'I think I'm going to swim in the freestyle and breaststroke events. What about you, Mickey? *Mickey!*'

But Mickey was in a dream. Jo followed his gaze over the Olympic-size outdoor pool, over the roofs of the town to the west, over the tops of the tall trees that grew between the school and the shore, and out across the wide blue sweep of the bay to the distant horizon.

'Mickey, snap out of it! You're thinking about Dana again, aren't you?'

'What...? Oh yeah, sorry, Jo. What did you say?'

'It doesn't matter. Look, I'd better get back to my team area – good luck!'

Mickey looked around him and saw that everyone was as enthusiastic as Jo. For the students and teachers alike, it was a day to get outside the classroom and into the sun. Students were milling around everywhere, trying to find their team areas, and a couple of boys were having a mock wrestling match on the lawn. Others were flicking wet towels at each other and trying to avoid being caught by their teachers.

Dominique was sitting directly opposite Mickey, having her hair brushed by a posse of her giggling girlfriends. Mickey tried to get her attention by waving at her. She didn't seem to notice him. Instead, he caught Jo's eye and she waved back frantically. Mickey smiled and drank in the atmosphere. At the finishing end of the pool, Mickey could see Miss Blythe, Mrs Reed and Mr Hird comparing stopwatches. They were the timekeepers for the day. Senior students who weren't competing were sitting at a table, ready to take down the results as they came in. At the starting blocks, Mr Crichton, Mickey's history teacher, had dropped his pistol into the pool and was desperately trying to fish it out before the caps went soggy.

The only person who seemed to have any control was Miss Hinson, the new sports teacher, who was pacing along the side of the pool, clipboard and pen at the ready, as befitted the judge of the events. She looked tanned and fit and was friendly and helpful to everyone. Mickey liked the look of her.

The tannoy announced that the High School Swimming Gala was about to begin!

'Would boys of thirteen and under, who wish to enter the fifty-metre freestyle event, please report to the marshalling area and see Miss Mullins. The marshalling area is situated between the boys' toilets and the canteen... Thank you!'

Mickey made his way over there. He felt quite relaxed about the day, and his laid-back attitude was partly a result of not knowing what to expect. He didn't even know if he was competitive or not. Until now, the only reason he swam was because he enjoyed it. He never swam at the pool because he'd always preferred the ocean, where the dolphins were.

As Mickey and his fellow classmates, now his rivals, approached the starting blocks, Mr Crichton was going over the rules.

'Now, boys, since it's your first time, I want you all to listen carefully. When I say "take your marks", I want you all to step on the back of the blocks. When I say "set", step to the front and get into a position to dive, and then wait for the sound of the starting pistol... oh, I mean whistle. When you hear the whistle – go!'

Before Mickey could really take in the instructions, they were already through the starting procedure and in the water, racing. He'd made a terrible start, but it didn't matter; within the first twenty metres of the race Mickey had pulled in front of everyone else! He was shooting through the water, legs thrashing and arms whirling like a demented egg whisk. He felt exhilarated.

As he swam, Mickey's vision was blurred by the cloudy water in the chlorinated pool. He could only see an arm's length ahead of him. All he was guided by were the black lane lines painted on the bottom of the pool. But that didn't matter; nothing could stop him. He didn't even take a breath until halfway through the race.

Students and teachers lined the sides of the pool, screaming and cheering the boys on. Jo found herself watching, along with the whole school, something truly amazing! Her best friend was swimming faster than anyone else in the water! She knew he was good, but she hadn't known he was that good. He was leaving the others standing!

As for Mickey, he couldn't hear the crowd; all he was aware of was the pounding of his heart and the rushing of the bubbles that swirled past his face. In the midst of this excitement, he began to hear the familiar clicks and squeaks that heralded Dana's approach. He couldn't believe that Dana was speaking to him while he was racing – it was like having his own personal coach urging him on.

'Swim as fast as you know
Speed of a dolphin you can go
In the water, fast and free
Go, Mickey, go! Swim like me!'

Dana continued to spur him on, but he didn't really need it; he was way out in the lead now. He surged on to win by six clear body lengths. He'd also smashed the school record – won eleven years before – by an incredible seven seconds!

Mickey had taken everyone by surprise, including himself. At first, everyone stood motionless, as if in shock, when Mickey finished the race. They were all overwhelmed by his performance – including the senior boys. Even they would have found it difficult to beat him if they'd been in the same race. Then the roar of the applause came, and one of the first to congratulate him was Jo.

'I can't believe it! You were fantastic, Mickey!' she gasped.

'Thanks, Jo. Guess what? Dana spoke to me and—'

But before Mickey could finish his sentence, he found himself surrounded by his classmates coming up to congratulate him. Jo was left wondering what he'd meant. But she never got the chance to talk to him again that afternoon because he was everyone else's hero.

Every time he swam, he heard Dana, and he won every event he entered! The breaststroke, the backstroke, even the butterfly event. But none was as impressive as that first freestyle race. It was that event which had captured everyone's attention, and no-one was more impressed by Mickey than the new sports instructor, Miss Hinson.

Judy Hinson was born and bred in the city and, shortly after graduating from teaching college, she was posted to Blue Rock High. As a teenager she had excelled in most sports, but her forte was swimming. After a lot of dedication and effort, Judy had become a semi-successful competitor, but she'd never really made the big time. She still had a passion for it, but she'd decided now to put all her experience into teaching. She loved her job, as was evident from the way she got along with her students. She was definitely a favourite with them and she seemed to have a knack for spotting the potential in a child, and then working to bring it out to the full. And today she saw her chance again – Mickey's talent was outstanding.

'Hey Mickey, wait a moment!' shouted Judy. He and Jo were heading for the school gates, on their way home.

'Yes, Miss Hinson?'

'Congratulations! You're a great swimmer.'

'Oh, thanks,' said Mickey, shyly.

'Have you ever competed before? Have you got a coach?'

'No, never, and I *sort* of have a coach,' said Mickey, immediately annoyed with himself for saying it.

Judy was determined to find out more. 'Sort of? Who?' she pressed.

'Well... she's a close friend of mine...' stammered Mickey.

'Does she live here in Blue Rock then?'

'No, not really...' Mickey looked at Jo who had an expression on her face that said, You're not going to tell her, are you?

Mickey tried his best to change the subject. 'You wouldn't know her, really!'

'Well, if she's involved in swimming, maybe I do. What's her name?' Judy really wanted to find out.

'Look... I've gotta go!' And without saying any more, Mickey ran off.

CHAPTER SEVEN

Confused and unsure of what had happened, Judy was left standing with Jo, trying to make sense of Mickey's sudden departure. Being new to the school and the town, Judy didn't know about Mickey's past. She decided to ask Jo and do a bit of research.

Jo talked about Mickey's life, including the accident, but she made sure she didn't mention Dana. As much as Mickey was protective of Dana, so was Jo of Mickey.

Later that evening, Judy called at Mickey's house to have a chat with him and his father. They were all sitting in the living room.

'It was kind of you to invite me in, Mr Nolan,' she said.

'Please, call me Terry. And it's a pleasure meeting you. Mickey hadn't mentioned he'd got a new sports teacher.'

Mickey sat and watched while his father and his sports teacher chatted to each other. They hardly seemed to notice him. Mickey hadn't seen his father so enthusiastic for a long time. And he hadn't seen him laugh as much either.

'Mr Nolan... Terry... Let me discuss the reason I came here in the first place. I really do believe that Mickey has the potential, and the talent, to be the first student from Blue Rock High to go all the way to the National Schools' Swimming Championships. And with your permission, and his coach's, I'd like him to spend some extra time after school each day to train. That's if Mickey's interested?'

Mickey jumped in. 'You bet!'

'Hold on!' interrupted Terry. 'Mickey's coach? Mickey doesn't have a coach! Mick, what's going on?'

Mickey sank into the sofa. Oh no! he thought. Judy caught Mickey's worried expression and she quickly covered up for him.

'Terry, that's my mistake. Did I say coach? How stupid of me! I must have been thinking of someone else. So, what do you think?'

Terry gave his permission without hesitating and went out to the kitchen to make Judy a cup of tea, leaving her alone with Mickey.

'Mickey, I want to apologize for prying this afternoon. It was none of my business. I hope you can forgive me?' she said, kindly.

Mickey couldn't believe it; this person was great! First she covered up for him, and then she apologized. If anyone ought to say they were sorry, it should be him, he thought. He was the one who had run away so rudely.

'I also want to let you know, Mickey, that if there's anything you want to talk about, *anything*, then I'm a very good listener. Whatever the subject – like your coach, for instance – I'm happy to talk.'

Mickey felt guilty. He had a strong urge to explain himself, but that would mean talking about Dana. He really liked Miss Hinson: he felt at ease with her, and unlike so many adults, Miss Hinson was treating him as an equal, and not talking down to him.

'Miss Hinson, if I tell you something special, something very personal and true to me, will you believe me?' asked Mickey.

'Well, it would depend, Mickey. I suppose if you truly believe it, then yes, I would have no choice but to respect you and believe in this special something as well.'

So Mickey decided to tell her. As he re-told the events leading up to his meeting with Dana, Judy sat dumbfounded. Mickey was just finishing his story as Terry returned with the tea.

Judy went on to explain the procedure that was needed to make it to the National Championships. She explained that Mickey would have to swim in a series of competitions leading up to the Nationals. Qualification for each competition was based on time. In other words, Mickey would have to do more than just *win* races. He would have to get fast enough times to secure a place in the subsequent competitions.

Although a little confused, Mickey and Terry listened intently.

'All you have to do, Mickey, is swim your fastest. Even if you look as if you're going to win comfortably, like you did today, don't hold back. Go all the way. Time is important – swim like a dolphin.' Smiling, Judy winked at Mickey. Terry obviously thought he'd missed something while he was out of the room.

'What have you two been talking about?' he asked.

Mickey replied by winking at his teacher. 'You bet!' was all he said.

So, for the next couple of weeks, under Miss Hinson's expert guidance, Mickey trained every day after school at the Blue Rock swimming pool. She made Mickey do different activities during the training sessions, to help build his strength and endurance in the water. At the beginning of each session, Judy timed Mickey sprinting the length of the pool. Not having anyone to compete against, Mickey found it difficult to push himself at times. But with each sprint, and as the days went on, he continued to break his personal best.

Judy was happy with the way Mickey was

progressing. His usual training sessions would consist of first, a six-lap warm-up at a gentle pace, followed by a number of laps swimming with a kickboard.

'Believe it or not, Mickey, kicking is a crucial part of swimming – keep going!' Judy yelled as she paced along the edge of the pool, watching Mickey's every stroke. As Mickey was a good sprinter, Judy would get him to do twelve half-pool sprints in succession, with a two-minute rest period in between. By the time Mickey got to the twelfth sprint, his arms felt as heavy as lead. In some pain, he had to strain to lift them, stroke after stroke. He ended each training session exhausted. But he never complained – he always did what Judy asked him to.

Sometimes, during the training, he would speak to Dana, but mostly their conversations were in the evenings when Mickey lay in bed, undisturbed by his normal daytime activities.

On very hot days, Mickey couldn't train because the pool was open to the public and was over-crowded. But most of the time a couple of lanes were put aside for those, like

Mickey, who wanted to swim laps. Then the other half of the pool was sectioned off for people who just wanted a dip, like Jo. She watched Mickey, and occasionally she'd wait for him to finish so they could walk back home together.

One afternoon, Dominique Peterson and her gang of girlfriends made a point of bumping into her.

'So, girls, this is where "uglies" like Jo Powell come to watch their sad boyfriends work out,' she hissed.

Jo didn't care what Dominique said about her, and normally she ignored this kind of encounter, but she wasn't going to let anyone bad-mouth Mickey.

'He's not sad! What would you know, anyway? Get a life, Peterson!'

'With your looks, that's what I should be saying to you!' The other girls giggled in unison. Dominique strutted off, posing as she went.

Jo groaned. That Dominique Peterson loved herself so much it was sickening. She yelled after her, 'Hey, Peterson! I've got a joke for you. What do you call ten Dominiques lined up together side by side? A wind tunnel!'

Dominique stood looking blankly at her. She obviously hadn't got it. Her friends all began to giggle again, until Dominique turned and gave them all a cold stare. Jo grinned at them.

As Mickey had finished his training, she ran over to him and he asked what all the fuss was about.

'Oh nothing,' said Jo, smiling. 'Just Dominique and I getting to know each other a little better.'

'Really!' said Mickey, interested. 'Maybe if you make friends with each other, I can get to know her a little better, too!'

Jo looked at Mickey, disappointed, and walked away with a toss of her head.

'What did I say?' shouted Mickey, naively.

At last, the first of the series of competitions had arrived. It was the Local District Zone Competition. Blue Rock High had a squad of twenty swimmers competing against six other schools in the surrounding district. The competition was to be held in the neighbouring town of Riversdale, about a forty-minute drive from Blue Rock.

By the end of that day, Mickey was a big success. It had been a carbon-copy of what had happened two weeks earlier. He'd won the breaststroke, backstroke and butterfly events but, as before, his most impressive win was in the fifty-metre freestyle. And just like the first time, he broke all the records. While he'd been swimming, Mickey had heard Dana's encouraging clicks and squeaks which had spurred him on to victory.

Two days later, as the results of the other district competitions came in, Miss Hinson made an announcement to the school that Mickey was the only one out of the entire Blue Rock High squad to qualify for the All-Zone Championships.

'Mickey, do you want the good news or the bad news first?' asked Judy, later. He smiled and she went on. 'Well, the bad news is that, unfortunately, even though you won, your times in the other events weren't good enough to qualify. But the good news is that you've qualified in the freestyle event as one of the favourites. So, All-Zone Championships, here we come!'

'Thanks, Miss Hinson!' Mickey was ecstatic. He couldn't wait to rush home and share the news with his dad... and Dana.

CHAPTER EIGHT

In no time at all, it was All-Zone Championship day. Mickey felt strange being the only representative from his High School – gone was the bus load of screaming fellow students. Instead, it was just him and Miss Hinson in her white Mini on the motorway, heading towards another competition, in another town.

'I don't want to put you off, Mickey, but today is going to be more competitive than the previous races. You'll be up against students who swim in organized competitions every weekend. Most of them belong to swimming clubs.'

Mickey knew what Miss Hinson was

telling him. He knew that at this competition he'd be racing against city kids from private schools: private schools which had the luxury of having their own indoor heated swimming pools, where their students could swim every day of the year, no matter what the weather was. He knew it was going to be tough – but he was ready for it.

'Don't worry, I'll be all right, Miss Hinson,' he smiled confidently at her.

'I'm sure you will, Mickey. I'm sure you will.'

Once they were at the competition, Judy was asked to be an official timekeeper, so Mickey was left to sit by himself for the day. There was even a designated area for him, with a sign saying 'Blue Rock students here'. A little embarrassed, Mickey sat himself beside the sign. He was stuck in between two major city schools. Both schools looked as though they had about fifty swimmers each! Soon, students from other schools realized that Mickey was the only representative from Blue Rock High. They began to laugh and giggle at him. Mickey just smiled at them – he could see the funny side himself. But as it was his first time, naturally he was feeling uncomfortable and slightly nervous.

As he looked around, he could see some teams even had their own cheerleading squads. There were banners and flags bearing school colours everywhere. There was more excitement and buzz at this competition than he'd ever experienced before. Mickey tried to block out the carnival atmosphere around him by reading the programme, but it was hard to ignore it. So instead he decided to sit and watch and wait until his event was called.

'Boys for the under-fourteen's fifty-metre freestyle, please report to the marshalling area,' said the tannoy.

It was time. Mickey began to make his way over. He turned back to see Miss Hinson waving at him and mouthing the words 'Go for it!' He smiled and waved back. As he was walking across to the pool side, he noticed that some students he'd just passed were giggling at him. Why are they laughing at me? he thought. Is there something wrong with me?

Once he was at the marshalling area, he'd

worked out what the big joke was: it was his football shorts. Mickey always swam in his football shorts. In the previous competitions, there had been plenty of boys who'd worn shorts. But it quickly dawned on Mickey that those boys, including himself, were non-competitive swimmers. Swimmers who belonged to a club and swam every weekend at organized competitions always wore competition briefs – or 'speedos' as they were called. Here everyone seemed to be wearing speedos. Mickey realized that out of the boys he was about to race, he was the only one wearing shorts. They had caps and goggles as well. Mickey hadn't worn a cap and goggles or a pair of speedos in his entire life.

Oh boy! he thought. These guys are serious! It's as though they're in the Olympics, or something. And by the way they strutted and paced about, staring at each other with a cocky arrogance, one could see that these boys were out to achieve one thing – to win.

'Hey, you!'

Mickey turned to see a tall red-haired kid standing behind him. By the way he was staring down at Mickey, he was obviously trying to intimidate him.

'Hey, you, I said! What's a nerd like you doing here? Hey, I'm talking to you, nerd-face!'

Mickey didn't answer him. He tried again. 'You with the pretty little shorts. Got something to hide, have you?' And with that, the bully proceeded to grab Mickey's shorts and pull them down to his knees. As fast as they went down, Mickey tried to pull them up again. Embarrassed, and with his pride bruised, Mickey turned to see the rest of the boys laughing at him and the bully howling hysterically.

Mickey was furious! He'd never felt as angry as he was feeling at that moment. It was as if a bomb was about to explode inside him. Before he knew it, he was pouncing on the other guy, throwing him to the ground.

The marshal was quickly at the scene.

'Hey! Break it up! I said break it up or you'll both be disqualified!' The two boys separated. 'If you two pull a stunt like that again, you'll both be banned from swimming in any high school competition again! Now listen carefully while I mark off the names for this event.'

As the official began to read out the names, the bully leaned over to Mickey. 'You'll keep!' he sneered.

'Lane four, Paul Galloway, City Grammar.'

'Here,' answered the red-head. Paul Galloway – that was a name Mickey wasn't going to forget in a hurry!

'Lane five, Mickey Nolan, Blue Rock High.'

Mickey answered.

Paul, to everyone's surprise, was *still* having a go at Mickey. 'Blue Rock? Where the heck is that? I bet you don't even have electricity. Have a nice doggy-paddle, you loser,' he snarled over his shoulder.

So the race had already begun – and there would be a loser, but Mickey was determined it wouldn't be him. What had started as a fight in the marshalling area continued as a battle in the water. It was obvious from the beginning of the race that this competition was between Paul and Mickey – the other boys didn't stand a chance. It was the toughest race either of them had entered. They were swimming evenly, side by side, and everyone, including the judges, looked nervous – this was going to be a close thing.

The pool was packed on either side with screaming students. The cheers were deafening and most of them were for Paul. His school even had a cheerleading squad chanting, 'Go, Paul! Go, Paul! GO! GO! GO!'

No-one knew who Mickey was, but he still had *some* support. Below the water, the squeaks and clicks of Dana were pushing him to go faster and faster, while above Judy was screaming her lungs out, even though she was being drowned out by the other chanting.

'Come on, Mickey! Come on!' She was so excited that she forgot to time the boy swimming in her lane.

With a metre to go, Mickey made an almighty effort, stretching for the wall, winning by a touch. He'd done it! He couldn't believe it was true – and neither could Paul.

'That was a fluke. I had a bad start. I'll beat you next time, nerd,' he hissed at Mickey. But

Mickey was too excited to notice. Later in the day, he found out that both he and Paul had qualified for the next competition: the major one just before the Nationals – the All-Schools' State Swimming Championship.

Waiting for Miss Hinson to finish her official duties for the day, Mickey was approached by a guy who said he was a journalist and he asked Mickey if he could interview him.

'That was an impressive swim, especially to beat those city swimmers,' he said. 'I've got a question for you. It says in the programme that you're from Blue Rock. You wouldn't be related to the Nolans who were involved in a boating accident a few years ago? I remember doing an article about it at the time.'

Mickey told the journalist that that was his family and the journalist couldn't believe his luck. 'This should make a lovely story – the fact that you nearly drowned as a child and now you're a strong swimmer, on your way to the State Championships! Wow! By the way, do you ever think about that dolphin that saved you?'

Mickey smiled. 'Yes, all the time!' he said.

'I must say, I love dolphins myself. Sometimes I've even dreamt about them,' the man said.

Why was this guy saying all this? thought Mickey. Was it just a coincidence or was he a very good journalist trying to find a sensational, Dana-like story? He seemed nice enough. And if he loved dolphins, then maybe he would understand about Dana.

'So, have you ever dreamt of dolphins, Mickey?' the journalist continued. That was it, thought Mickey. That question was too close to home. Mickey decided he would finish the interview there and then. He didn't want to say too much to this man. He was a journalist after all. Just then, Mickey remembered a song that Dana had sung to him the previous night. At the time he hadn't understood it.

'Live and learn and you will know
What's in your heart won't hurt to show
If it's true, you can confide
Live and believe, no need to hide.'

Mickey repeated the last line to himself...
'no need to hide'.

'What did you say?' asked the journalist.

'Nothing! No, nothing really. Well... I'd
like to talk to you about a friend of mine,' said
Mickey, and he proceeded to tell the journalist
all about Dana. From across the pool, Judy
could see Mickey and the journalist chatting
for ages.

The next morning, the whole of Blue Rock
was talking about Mickey. He was in the
national papers. He was an instant celebrity.
Over breakfast, Mickey and Jo were reading
out the articles to each other.

'Mickey, they're calling you Dolphin Boy
Blue.' And Jo read out a passage from one of
the newspapers:

> '"The boy hails from the coastal
> town of Blue Rock. As a child, he
> was allegedly saved by a dolphin
> in a boating accident, and he
> now claims to talk to a dolphin
> in his dreams. Whatever the

case, this Dolphin Boy Blue has made it to the All-State Schools' Swimming Championships."'

'Well, listen to this one.' Mickey was reading another article.

'"A thirteen-year-old from the small town of Blue Rock has qualified for his All-Schools' State Swimming Championships and is tipped for the National Finals. With no previous background in competition swimming, it seems he has made it with pure raw talent and motivation. But, he claims, he also has the support of a special friend – a dolphin!"'

'This is so cool, Mickey, you're famous! But I didn't think you were going to tell anyone about Dana, and now the whole country knows! What did your dad say?'
'Dana convinced me I had nothing to hide.

I believe in her, and if no one else does, then it's their problem. And yeah, Dad was upset with me for mentioning Dana, but that was no surprise. It doesn't matter anyway, the newspaper people got that part wrong. They said that Dana was in my dreams, when the truth is she's not.'

At school, Mickey and Jo were swamped by students wanting to talk to Mickey. Some even wanted his autograph. Mickey was, indeed, a hero.

CHAPTER NINE

For the next couple of weeks leading up to the State Championships, Mickey was the most popular kid in school. His new-found fame also brought him many new 'friends'. People who didn't talk to him before, like Dominique Peterson and her group, were now hanging out with him.

'So, will you be interviewed again, Mickey?' asked Dominique. She and her friends were gathered round Mickey, standing in the school corridor.

'Probably,' said Mickey. 'I gave an interview last night over the phone – for a sports magazine.'

'This is so *exciting*! And I think it's so cute

that you dream of dolphins. That's my favourite fish you know,' simpered Dominique.

'Well, they're not fish, they're mammals and it's not actually a dream... ' Mickey paused and decided not to go on. He didn't want to tell the whole story to Dominique, even though he relished all the attention he was getting from her and her friends.

'Hope you can sit with us again at lunch time, Mickey.' She smiled at him.

'Yeah, I will. See you then, Dominique.'

As the girls made their way to class, Mickey turned to see Jo at the end of the corridor, heading his way. He hadn't seen her for a couple of days. He called to her, but she didn't acknowledge him. It dawned on Mickey that she might be ignoring him on purpose.

'Hey, Jo!' he said, falling into step beside her. 'Where have you been for the last couple of days?'

'I've been around. You just haven't noticed me, that's all!'

'What do you mean, Jo?' He looked puzzled.

'You know what I mean,' she said, shrugging.

Mickey could tell that Jo was upset as she went on, 'You haven't seen me around because you've been too busy with your new friends, like Dominique Peterson and her airhead mates.'

Mickey was hurt by what Jo was saying, even though deep down he knew it was true. He *had* been distracted by all the attention and, in the process, Jo had been pushed into the background. Mickey was embarrassed and felt guilty but he wasn't going to admit he was in the wrong. Instead, he defended his actions by telling Jo she was being over-sensitive.

'You're just jealous because Dominique's talking to me,' he said.

'I am *not*! And the only reason she's talking to you is because your photo's in the papers!'

'That's not true!' Mickey insisted.

'Oh, wake up, Mickey, don't be so blind.' They were both shouting now. The argument was going nowhere and it soon ended with both Mickey and Jo storming off in opposite directions.

Later in the day, they bumped into each other again. Jo was the first to apologize.

'Look, I'm sorry about what I said earlier. We haven't been swimming at the beach for a while – do you wanna go after school?'

'Yeah, you bet... Oh, I can't.' Mickey remembered that he'd planned to go over to Dominique's house after school with her.

'Why not?' asked Jo. 'I know you haven't got training – it's your night off.'

'Yeah, but I still have to meet Miss Hinson to talk about swimming tactics and stuff.'

'Oh well, I'll see you later then. Bye.' And she was gone.

It was the first time Mickey had lied to Jo and he hated doing it. He felt so annoyed with himself that, in the end, he broke his date with Dominique and decided to wander around the shops in Blue Rock instead.

Head down and with his hands in his pockets, Mickey moped along the street. People passing by recognized him and said hello, but he was deep in thought and hardly noticed them at all.

Just then, he recognized a shop he had just passed. It was the place where Jo had got his birthday present! He'd never been in there before, so he went back to take a closer look. The sign on the door said 'Back in ten minutes'. Mickey put his face against the window and peered in. He could see a lot of books and hand-painted greetings cards. There were crystals everywhere, some hanging and others in a glass cabinet. And there was a sign on the wall saying *Have your palm read by Madam Karma*. It all looked very unusual.

Mickey had heard many things about Madam Karma. Some people in the town thought she was a bit strange, even though they didn't know her personally. He'd heard that she spoke to ghosts and spirits, too! Some of the kids at school thought she was a real live witch, brewing up spells all the time. Mickey didn't know what to believe. If that was true, then she was probably a little old lady dressed in black with long, tangled black and grey hair, black bushy eyebrows, and warts on her nose. The whole works! thought Mickey.

'Hello. Are you interested in buying something?'

'Aaagh!' Mickey nearly jumped out of his

skin. He turned to see a lady standing behind him – it was the same one he'd bumped into on the pier.

'I'm sorry, I didn't mean to startle you. I just wondered whether you're interested in buying something? This is my shop.'

'*You're* Madam Karma?'

'Yes. You seem surprised,' she said, smiling. She was right, he was.

'I know who *you* are. We met each other on the pier the other week. You're the boy who's made it to the State Swimming Championships, the one who talks to a dolphin in his dreams. You're Dolphin Boy Blue. It's Mickey, isn't it?' Mickey nodded. 'Why don't you come in and have a look around?'

'Look, I don't want to be rude or anything but I'm not into all that weird stuff,' said Mickey, feeling slightly uneasy.

'My dear pet, what's weird? Is that dolphin pendant around your neck weird? Some people may say talking to a dolphin in your dreams is weird, but we both know it isn't, don't we? Come on, come in.'

She'd made her point and Mickey decided to follow her. She invited him into her flat which was attached to the back of the shop.

'Please, make yourself comfortable. I'll put the kettle on. I'm dying to hear more about you and your dolphin experience.'

Mickey wasn't sure if he was dying to tell her, though. He was searching for something to say as Madam Karma rattled through the cupboards for tea cups and spoons.

'So, are you a fake?' Mickey blurted out. He winced. What was he *thinking*? It wasn't meant to come out like that! Mickey hoped she hadn't heard him. But she had.

'No. Are you?' she said, calmly.

Mickey defended himself. 'Of course not!'

'Then neither am I, pet,' she said. Mickey noticed that Madam Karma always said 'pet' in a very theatrical way. 'Don't be embarrassed, pet. There are many of us in this business who aren't genuine. But I like to think I am.'

Madam Karma went on to explain that, from a very early age, she'd had a gift for predicting things and events long before they happened. Nowadays she just gave crystal ball readings to friends. It was only recently that she'd begun to do palm readings, and she confessed she was still learning.

'My main job is running this store. Apart from selling things like crystals and meditation cassettes, I do sell a wide range of other things.'

Mickey looked about the flat and noticed numerous books about plants and wildlife.

'My friend Jo, who bought me this pendant, said the lady who served her knew a lot about dolphins. Was that you?' he asked.

'Yes, it was, but I don't claim to know everything about them. I don't think any person can. But I do know a few things.'

'Such as?' Mickey was curious to find out how much she knew, even though nothing would compare with how much he'd already learnt about dolphins from talking to Dana.

'Well, pet, you tell me about your dolphin and in return I'll tell you how much I know.'

It was a deal. Mickey told her his story of Dana, as he had with Jo, his father and the journalist. As he did so, Madam Karma kept refilling his cup. As he spoke, he could see that Madam Karma was listening carefully, taking in every word he said. She sat there and smiled at him, as she had the day they'd met on the pier.

'My dear, that is wonderful. You're so lucky that Dana has come to you. I knew you were special. Dolphins are the most wonderful creatures on earth. There is so much we can learn from them. Your story is like all the stories that have ever been told about the bond between man and dolphin.'

'Other stories?' asked Mickey.

'Oh yes, pet!' said Madam Karma. She was getting excited. 'For centuries different cultural groups around the world have told their own special tales about dolphins, just like you have. In fact, you said that everyone thinks that you're dreaming of Dana, but you claim she's very real and that you're speaking to her, mind to mind. Well, did you know that I know stories of people in the same position as you, who have been speaking to dolphins, telepathically, for hundreds of years.'

'You *do*?' Mickey was on the edge of his

seat. He knew Dana had said that dolphins had made contact with other people, but she'd never said who.

'There are a group of aborigines in Northern Australia called the Wurunjeri tribe. They're sometimes known as the "Dolphin People". The elders of the tribe claim to speak to the dolphins, mind to mind – just like you with Dana. The dolphins give them advice on tribal issues. The Dolphin People believe that, when they die, their spirits return to the dolphins in the ocean to be protected by them in the afterlife, just as they were in their life on earth. They feel that to kill a dolphin is like killing one of themselves. They also believe that the dolphins are the creatures closest to the human race.'

Mickey was stunned. He was impressed with Madam Karma's knowledge. He wanted to know more. Not even Dana had shared any specific stories with him.

Madam Karma went on. 'Let me tell you about one particular legend: this time it comes from the Ancient Greeks. It's about a young musician named Arion. Once upon a time... '

Arion sat strumming his harp, making beautiful music. But on this particular day his heart was not in it. He was sad and in need of cheering up.

'Servant!' he called. Arion was very famous and wealthy. 'Fetch me the finest fruit around!'

The servant came back with a platter of the most exotic and delicious fruit in the district. After eating every single piece, Arion was still feeling depressed.

'Servant, I would like some dancing girls to perform for me'

So the servant came back with the best dancing troupe seen for miles and miles. They danced for two hours but still Arion wasn't feeling any better.

Finally, the servant approached Arion and said, 'My talented master, if you do not mind me asking, why are you feeling so sad?'

'It has been many years since I have been away from my birthplace. I believe I am suffering from home sickness. I long to be back home, in Corinth.'

'Then, if my master doesn't mind my

saying so, why do you not go back?' There was a pause. The servant worried that perhaps he shouldn't have put forward his opinion. It was something servants never did. But Arion was a compassionate man and he treated all his servants fairly.

'My dear friend, you are right! There is nothing to stop me from going home.'

So Arion hired a ship and set sail for Corinth. Once he and his crew were out at sea, and almost half way through their journey, Arion began to feel happier. He knew he would be home very soon. On deck, he looked out at the endless blue horizon and dreamt of his family. But down below, his crew were scheming.

'So, you all know the plan,' said the captain. 'Tonight we will kill him and his money will be ours. We will be rich!' The crew roared their agreement.

That evening, as planned, they grabbed Arion.

'What is the meaning of this?' he shouted, frightened. He struggled to free himself, but it was no use. Four men pinned him down. The leader approached Arion with a long, sharp knife and placed it inches away from Arion's throat.

'Musician,' the leader snarled. 'It is time for you to say goodbye!' He raised his arm ready to kill poor Arion.

'STOP!' yelled Arion. 'Doesn't a man about to die have a final request?'

'A final request?' The leader looked at the others. They laughed and agreed that they were men enough to let him have his wish. 'Of course you can, and what is your final request, may I ask?' the leader sniggered.

'To do what I have done passionately all my life; to play my harp and sing for the last time,' pleaded Arion.

Freed from the bonds that tied him, and on deck ready to play his last concert, Arion looked up at the night sky and prayed for a way to get out of his predicament. But his barbaric audience was getting restless.

'Hurry up, musician! We haven't got all night, and neither have you!' They shouted with laughter.

Arion began his song. It was like a hymn –

soft and sad. The crew were still rowdy. As Arion reached the final bars of the song, he looked over his shoulder and saw the dark ocean crashing against the ship. When the song ended, Arion made his move.

As he leapt up, the captain and his crew rushed at him, and Arion threw his precious instrument at them, in defence. With nowhere else to go, Arion flung himself overboard. The last thing he heard before he fell into the water was the captain shouting:

'You fool! To die by the knife would have been less painful than to be eaten by sharks!'

The ship sailed into the darkness. Arion was left bobbing about in the black ocean. He was certain he was going to die. But just then, underneath him, a large dolphin wedged himself against Arion. And before long, Arion was being carried to safety on the back of this dolphin. Once they got to the shore, the dolphin swam silently away and, eventually, Arion continued his journey back to Corinth.

When at last he arrived at his home, Arion wrote a song about his ordeal. He wrote, thanking Poseidon, god of the oceans, for sparing his life. He also wrote about the love that dolphins have for music. Arion believed that it was his music that attracted the dolphin which saved him. The gods rewarded the dolphin by placing its image within the stars forever. Later, this constellation would be known as Delphinus – or The Dolphin.

CHAPTER TEN

'Did you know that up there in the sky is the constellation of a dolphin, called Delphinus – thanks to a guy named Arion? Trouble is, we can't see it in Australia, because it can only be seen in the Northern Hemisphere.'

'What are you talking about?' Jo wasn't sure what Mickey was trying to tell her as they made their way to school the next day. Mickey couldn't stop thinking about the meeting he'd had with Madam Karma. They had talked and talked well into the evening.

'How did the meeting go with Miss Hinson?' asked Jo.

'Meeting? Oh, the meeting.' Mickey remembered the lie he'd told Jo. 'Yeah, it went

OK. It didn't last long. After that, I wandered around the shops.'

'Hey, there's the woman I bought your present from.' Jo had spotted Madam Karma across the road, sweeping the path in front of her shop.

'That's Madam Karma,' explained Mickey.

'*She's* Madam Karma?' answered Jo, surprised. 'When I bought the pendant, I didn't realize that was her. You know, some kids at school think she's a real live witch and—'

'Just silly rumours, Jo.' Mickey ran across the street, calling out a big, 'Hi ya!'

'Hi ya?' Jo was getting confused now. 'How does *he* know her?' She crossed the road to meet her properly.

Jo had taken an instant liking to Madam Karma. She was so beautiful, she thought.

'So, what do you think? It looks good on him, doesn't it, pet?' Madam Karma was pointing to the dolphin pendant around Mickey's neck. Jo just smiled and nodded. 'Would you like to come in for a cuppa?' she said, still looking at Jo.

'Thanks, but school starts in fifteen

minutes,' said Mickey.

'Well, what about later, after school?'

Mickey explained that he couldn't, because of swimming practice, but he convinced Jo that she should. He looked at his friend as if to say 'she's OK'.

Hesitantly, Jo said, 'All right, thanks. I'll see you after school then.'

'Hello, is anyone around?' Jo shouted, as she waited at the counter in Madam Karma's store.

'Come right through, pet. I'm at the back.'

There, sitting in her flat with a pot of tea, cups and saucers, and chocolate biscuits neatly arranged on a china plate, was Madam Karma.

'Come in, love, don't be shy. Sit yourself down. I've been looking forward to your visit all day. Milk? Sugar?'

Jo was on her best behaviour. 'Yes, please. One spoonful, thank you.'

In fact, to begin with Jo didn't say very much. Madam Karma was very outgoing and certainly had 'the gift of the gab'. They started off chatting about general things – like the weather, the sort of people who came into the shop, Jo's favourite subjects at school, and stuff like that.

'And tell me, if you don't mind me asking, do you a have boyfriend?' asked Madam Karma.

Jo blushed. 'Oh no! Not really.'

'That's a shame. I think you and Mickey look great together.' Jo blushed again. 'I didn't mean to embarrass you, pet, but you do like him, don't you? I wouldn't blame you, I think he's gorgeous myself.'

Jo just nodded, afraid she would say the wrong thing. She'd never told anyone how she really felt about Mickey. She loved him more than just a friend and wished, more than anything, that one day they could be together. She could always dream about it, but she knew that it could never be – Mickey just never thought of her like that.

'You know, I can see that you and Mickey will be together for a long time,' Madam Karma was saying.

'You can?' asked Jo

'Of course! But sometimes you just can't rely on fate alone. Sometimes you have to create your own destiny. You need to give it a good kick up the backside to get it going!' Jo smiled. Madam Karma poured her another cup of tea.

'Mickey's very lucky to have you around. Young love is wonderful. I remember— '

Jo hadn't confessed her feelings about Mickey to Madam Karma. There was no need to. She'd guessed it for herself. All Jo could do was continue to blush and listen.

'I remember when I was young – not quite as young as you – in my early twenties... Well, I can show you!'

Madam Karma went to the cabinet which was standing in the corner of the living room, and pulled a black and white photo of herself out of a drawer. Jo couldn't believe it! She was stunning. She thought she looked like one of those old-time movie stars – like Marilyn Monroe.

Madam Karma continued. 'That photo was taken in my acting days. Yes, I wanted to be a famous actress. I was living in London at the time, desperate to get a part as a leading lady on the West End stage. But as it turned out I was only ever a chorus girl in a couple of musicals. In spite of all that, it was the best time of my life, because that's when I met the man of my dreams. Oh, I'm sorry, I must be boring you to tears.'

'No, please go on,' said Jo, fascinated.

Madam Karma went on to tell Jo of a good-looking young actor she'd met when they'd had to read a part together. She'd been so overwhelmed by him – really love at first sight – that she'd given him a passionate kiss during their audition. Needless to say, the director hadn't been too impressed as the script hadn't called for a kiss, and she'd felt so embarrassed herself that she'd never told the young man how she'd really felt about him; even when she'd seen him, months later, in a café with his friends. It was something she'd always regretted.

'The point is, pet,' Madam Karma was saying now, 'that whenever you have the opportunity to let someone know how you really feel about them – like Mickey – don't be scared. Tell them! Grab your chance!'

Jo knew that Madam Karma was right, but

she didn't want to risk her friendship with Mickey. For the first time, she found herself expressing how she really felt about him.

'You see, there's nothing I want more than to be Mickey's girlfriend, but I know he looks on me as his best mate – or even his sister, sometimes. I just wish there was some way of knowing that there might be a chance we'd be together, eventually.'

'Well, pet, you've come to the right place,' said Madam Karma. 'It's my business to find out what might happen.'

Madam Karma asked Jo to give her something personal, like a watch or a bracelet. Though Jo felt quite sceptical – it was something she'd only seen done on TV – she was curious. She took off her watch and Madam Karma held it tightly in her hand. Her eyes were closed and she was concentrating hard.

She didn't say a word for a minute or so, then she said, 'Yes, I'm starting to see something.'

'What?' asked Jo, breathlessly.

'I can see Mickey and I can see you there as

well. It's not too clear, but it looks as though he's giving you some kind of sign: a sign which shows you that he cares about you.'

'Really?' Jo jumped up, excited now.

'I can see that there are other people looking at Mickey, too, but this sign is directed only at you.'

'What is it? What's the sign?' Jo couldn't contain herself any longer.

'I can't see. I'm losing focus. All I know is that you'll recognize it when you see it, pet.'

Jo felt stunned. That was all she wanted to hear. She thanked Madam Karma for the tea and the wonderful chat. She'd made a new friend in Madam Karma. All Jo had to do now was wait for the sign!

CHAPTER ELEVEN

Two weeks went by and now it was the State Championships. Dolphin Boy Blue was in the headlines more than ever. He'd qualified as the only student from a country school in his event, and it was up to Mickey to do his best for them now.

The competition was held at the State Swimming Centre, in the state's capital city, a two and a half hour drive east of Blue Rock. Once there, Mickey was amazed by the magnificent swimming complex. It would be the first time he'd swum in an indoor heated pool; a pool where, every morning, Olympic swimmers trained; a pool which had electronic devices, so that the times of each competitor could be screened on a huge digital scoreboard for everyone to see; a pool which you could go underneath and alongside, in a tunnel, and see the swimmers underwater, through huge glass windows.

Like the All-Zone competition, the carnival atmosphere was electrifying. The cheers and screams seemed even more deafening this time, as they echoed throughout the enclosed stadium. Once again, it was only Mickey and Miss Hinson from Blue Rock. Terry wanted to be there but couldn't because of work commitments, and Jo couldn't come along because she had to be at school. But this time, Miss Hinson wasn't needed as an official, so she sat beside Mickey for the entire competition.

Also there, loud as ever with his off-putting remarks, was Mickey's rival, Paul Galloway. He was still teasing Mickey about his shorts. Mickey had had the chance to get speedos when Miss Hinson offered to buy a pair for him, but he'd declined, saying he felt comfortable in his shorts.

'I'm not going to change just because I

don't look like other swimmers. I'm from Blue Rock and everyone from Blue Rock wears shorts,' he said.

As in the previous competition, the battle was really between Mickey and Paul. Both were cutting through the water very quickly but, as she watched, Judy remembered thinking that Mickey hadn't looked his usual self that day. It was also the first time that Mickey couldn't hear Dana's clicks and squeaks during the race. In the end, Paul beat him into second place, but his time was, just by the narrowest of margins, good enough to get him into the Nationals.

Mickey was disappointed with his swim. 'What went wrong?' he asked Miss Hinson, puzzled. She put it down to nerves and not being used to the indoor pool, but Mickey knew it wasn't that.

Eventually, Dana expressed her views.

'The truth can hurt, we often know
But when sung by friends, it's caring they
show.'

'Yes, but I should've won, Dana!'

*'Be always happy for what you have and
who you are
From then until now, you have come so far.'*

'I am! Don't get me wrong, I am!' insisted
Mickey.

Then Dana asked him what he was
thinking of, just before the race. She thought
that Mickey might not be focused enough.

'I was thinking about beating that big-
mouth, Paul Galloway,' said Mickey.

Dana replied:

*'All you could think was how the other
thought
You put focus on how the battle be fought
Swim your own race, that you should do
Forget the other, to yourself be true
You didn't picture me, that was the thing
With him on your mind, you can't hear
me sing
When you swim again, forget the rest
Believe only in self, give always your best.'*

Mickey understood what Dana meant. He took her advice and made a promise to her and to himself that he would be more focused for the Nationals.

The next morning, Mickey woke up to find Miss Hinson was in the house talking to his father. Mickey leapt out of bed to join them. They were discussing plans for the next three weeks, leading up to the Nationals. They all agreed that, since Blue Rock Pool had recently closed for another season, and it was now far too cold to swim in the surf, Mickey should move to the city. There, he could be trained in a heated pool by Judy's old coach, Tom Davies. He would have to do his school work by correspondence.

At first, Mickey was hesitant about the move, but he realized if he was going to give himself any chance against the city swimmers, he would have to go. And it meant that he would be further away from Dana, but at least they could still speak to each other, mind to mind. Almost right away, Mickey was packing his suitcase with Terry standing in the doorway.

'You know I'm proud of you, son. And I know your mother would be, too.' Mickey stopped packing. His father looked serious and Mickey could tell he was building up to something.

'You know, it's been hard to accept your story about this Dana, and recently I've been trying to understand it. You said that she's out in the bay – well, yesterday, some other fishermen spotted a dolphin.'

Mickey jumped with excitement. 'It's Dana, it's Dana, I know it is! Please, Dad, you've gotta let me go out on the boat.'

'Hold on, hold on. That's what I'm getting at. You must promise me that if we go out and don't see the dolphin, you'll be OK about it.'

'I promise,' pleaded Mickey, hysterically.

And so his father agreed to lift the ban. Mickey was ecstatic. He hugged his dad. It had been a long time since the two of them had hugged each other.

Before Miss Hinson came by to collect Mickey to take him to the city, Terry, three fisherman, Jo and Mickey were all out on a boat circling Blue Rock Bay. Mickey couldn't stop smiling. But Terry still wasn't sure if he'd done the right thing.

'Now don't get your hopes up, Mick. There's no guarantee that the dolphin will be out there.'

'She will, Dad, she will! It's not a dream. She's real!'

The fishermen steered the boat to the same location they'd spotted the dolphin the day before. But this time there was no sign of her. They tried a couple of other locations – again, nothing. After an hour searching most of the bay, Terry was ready to head back home. But Mickey wasn't giving up.

'Please, Dad, I know she's out here! We still haven't tried around the mouth of the bay. Please!'

Terry stared intensely at Mickey for a moment. They both knew that was the area they'd had the accident ten years before – where Mickey's mum had drowned.

'OK. We'll go there, but it's the last area we'll look and then we're heading home. Agreed?'

'Agreed! Thanks, Dad!'

As they headed towards the mouth of the bay, Mickey closed his eyes.

'What are you doing?' asked Jo.

'Sshh! I'm concentrating. I'm trying to call Dana.'

Once at the spot, everyone on the boat, except Mickey, looked about – there wasn't a dolphin in sight. Mickey still had his eyes closed. As the boat was chugging slowly through the choppy water, Terry decided it was time to head back in. All of a sudden, Mickey began to hear clicks and squeaks. He jumped up, eyes wide open, shouting.

'It's Dana! She's down below us, beneath the waves.'

'Where?' Neither Terry, Jo or the fishermen could see Dana anywhere. Without any warning, Mickey took a running jump and leapt overboard, clothes and all, into the cold grey ocean.

Jo screamed, 'Mickey!'

'Quick, turn the boat around!' shouted Terry. What was Mickey thinking of? He's finally gone crazy, thought Terry.

'Look! It's Dana!' yelled Jo.

As they steered the boat towards Mickey, they all stared in amazement. Mickey was swimming with a wild dolphin, far out in the middle of the ocean. Jo couldn't keep back her emotions as she laughed and cried with joy.

'Well, Terry, I guess your son really *is* a dolphin boy.'

Terry couldn't answer the fisherman. Overwhelmed by the whole affair, he'd just realized something that had been growing steadily ever since Mary's death: life does go on – it was happening right in front of him. His wife was gone, and it was finally time for him to let go and move on. The tears welled in his eyes as he sat and witnessed his son and the dolphin having their beautiful reunion.

CHAPTER TWELVE

'Well, we've finally made it.' Judy and Mickey pulled up in front of Tom Davies' house. Tom was outside, waiting to greet them.

'So, you must be Mickey Nolan. I've heard a lot of good things about you,' he said, smiling.

'Thanks, sir,' said Mickey, politely.

'Hey, if you're going to be living with me, I won't be having any of this 'sir' business. Just call me Tom.'

Mickey liked Tom instantly, and vice versa. He was a tough but kind man. He lived by himself now, since his wife had passed away a few years before, and he had three children who were all grown up and married. A short and stocky man, with a bit of a belly, he always wore a brown cardigan, checked shirt and brown corduroy trousers. He had short, silver hair and a big salt-and-pepper moustache.

After Mickey had settled in, Judy said her goodbyes and headed back to Blue Rock. Mickey and Tom were left alone to get to know each other.

'Are you hungry? Would you like something to eat?' asked Tom.

'No thanks, we ate McDonald's on the way.'

'McDonald's, huh? Well, that'll be the last bit of junk food you'll have until after the Nationals. I'm putting you on a very strict diet consisting of complex carbohydrates. I hope you enjoy food like pasta, potatoes and bananas?' Mickey nodded. He wasn't going to argue. Tom sounded like he knew what he was talking about.

'Well, if you've eaten, I think it's time to hit the sack. We have an early start tomorrow.'

Mickey looked at his watch. Tom must be kidding? It was only seven-thirty in the evening! Normally, Mickey wouldn't go to bed for at least another couple of hours.

'How early?' asked Mickey.

'Well, I've set the alarm for five-thirty. We have to be at the pool by six.'

Mickey learnt later that it was going to be like that every morning! He was put into a strict training programme. In fact, he was to swim for the next two weeks, twice a day, every day, excluding Sunday – which was his rest day.

For the period leading up to the Nationals, Mickey's life was timetabled. In a letter to Jo, he wrote down what his days consisted of.

Dear Jo

You won't believe how early we have to get up – usually it's around 5.30am! Even though I have an alarm, Tom still needs to wake me. Now I know how Dad feels when he gets up to go fishing. It's tough. Quarter of an hour later, I'm fully dressed and in the car with Tom. It only takes ten minutes to get to the pool, so I usually have a banana to eat and a small bottle of orange juice along the way. As soon as we get there, I change into my shorts (no, I still don't want to wear a pair of speedos!). I'm using goggles now, but only because I started to get sore eyes in the chlorinated water. I'm still not sure if I'll wear them in the race. By 6am, we're in the water training. Tom also coaches other swimmers. There are six boys and five girls in the squad. I'm the youngest. Tom sometimes gets me racing the older guys. It's tough work, but I love it!

After about an hour and a half of work, we finish up and head back to Tom's house to have breakfast. This is my favourite part of the day. I can't wait to eat after training! Most mornings I have cereal, three wholemeal muffins with sliced banana and honey on top, and sometimes a boiled egg.

After breakfast I have to start on my school work. Tom sometimes helps. (By the way, have you finished your history project yet?)

Then it's lunch! Usually, I have toasted tomato or chicken sandwiches. Some days Tom cooks up a rice dish. He's not a bad cook. In the afternoons I have to have a rest. Yeah, I know, but Tom thinks I should have a nap each day. I think it's more for him than me! Then school work again for an hour or so - Tom's very strict and he makes me do it.

We get back to the pool again by about 4pm. We only train for an hour. By 5pm it's time for dinner. Tom makes a mean spaghetti bolognaise! Then I get to watch TV or talk to Tom. We do that a lot — talk. We're really good friends. He knows about Dana and I think he understands.

Jo, did you know he nearly made it to the Olympics? Well, he told me that when he was twenty he was the favourite to win his event at the Olympic trials. If he'd won, it would've meant an automatic place in the 1956 Olympics. But an hour before the Olympic trials were set to begin, Tom was saying goodbye to his girlfriend. It was the last time they were seeing each other — she was moving to another city with her family. After the emotional goodbyes, Tom headed back to the pool but by the time he got there, it was too late! He'd missed his race by a whisker and his one chance to go to the Olympics was gone. Later, he learnt that his girlfriend had been killed when the bus she was travelling on had been involved in an accident. She died instantly. He gave up swimming after that and became a coach and later he met and married someone else. What a story, huh? I feel sorry for him. I hope I can win the Nationals for him.

Before I go to bed I call Dad (or you – it's your turn to call me!) and by that time, I'm ready for bed!

Anyway, now you know how busy I am, I'll say goodbye.

Love, Mickey.

It was certainly a hectic schedule and, as much as Mickey loved it, by the time each evening came round he was exhausted. He was so tired he found it difficult to talk to Dana. He tried to concentrate and tune into Dana's clicks and squeaks, but after a few minutes lying on his bed he would fall into a deep sleep. And the distance between Blue Rock and the city didn't help them either. In the past week, Mickey had only spoken to Dana twice;

once, while training in the pool, and the other when he was in bed. This worried Mickey – not being able to speak to his special friend. He really missed her, and everyone back at Blue Rock.

'Hey, Mickey! It's your dad.' Tom handed Mickey the phone.

'Hi, Dad. I'm great, but I miss home... Yeah, I know. Have you seen Dana? Well, maybe she's gone further out to sea. I hope she's OK. We're having curry tonight. Oh, I almost forgot, I'm going to be on TV on Friday night, on *The Andy Ball Show.* Yeah, I know Tom said no more interviews, but he's allowing just this one, so tell Jo. Yeah, of course I'm going to tell them about Dana. Look, don't worry, Dad. OK, love you, too.'

Friday night arrived and it seemed as though the whole of Blue Rock had found out about Mickey's appearance on national television. Everyone was glued to their TV sets. Jo was with Terry.

'Quick, Mr Nolan, it's about to begin!' she shouted, excitedly.

As the theme music of *The Andy Ball Show*

played, Mickey couldn't believe he was sitting there, in a television studio, in front of cameras and a live audience, about to be interviewed. He was feeling rather nervous.

'Hi, and welcome to *The Andy Ball Show*! And I'm Andy Ball, of course!' The audience applauded and cheered. Mickey watched as Andy went through his usual introduction and corny jokes. To be truthful, Mickey wasn't a fan of Andy Ball's – he always thought he appeared too false.

'Well, tonight our first guest is a very special young swimmer. The papers are calling him Dolphin Boy Blue. His name is Mickey Nolan and he comes from the small coastal town of Blue Rock. He's the only one in his event who's from the country, and he's made it all the way to the National Schools' Swimming Championships, which will be televized live next Tuesday on this network. Why's that so special? Well, his motivation for making it to the Nationals has come from a dolphin. Yes, a dolphin! Mickey claims that a dolphin, in the bay at Blue Rock, speaks to him telepathically. Sounds weird? Let's make him feel welcome – Mickey Nolan!'

The audience applauded. Then Mickey started to tell his story. The studio audience began to giggle. Mickey soon realized that Andy wasn't really interested in his story. In fact, he was sending up the whole interview and making it into a big joke. Tom was sitting in the audience, looking uncomfortable. He regretted that he'd let Mickey go on the show.

Back home, Terry and Jo were getting upset as they watched, too.

'That idiot is trying to make fun of my son,' said Terry.

Andy Ball carried on. 'So, let me recap – it's not a dream. You really do speak to a dolphin, mainly at bedtime. Well, viewers, that certainly gives a whole new meaning to the phrase "pillow talk".' The studio audience laughed. 'So what do your parents think?'

'Well, my father believes me. He's seen Dana, too. My mum died and I miss her a lot. I wish she was right here with me now. Dad said she was really good at knowing people. Knowing if they were *fake* or not.'

Suddenly, Andy felt uneasy and began to

look guilty. He knew Mickey had directed that comment at him, and so did the audience. Some of them started to cheer – Andy Ball was a loudmouth who needed to be put in his place. Mickey seemed to be doing that all by himself. Gradually, he was winning over the studio audience and the viewers, too.

Mickey went on, 'I know it must sound weird, but it's the truth. I'm so lucky Dana speaks to me. She's my best friend. Whenever I really wish I had my mum to talk to, I talk to Dana. She makes me feel better.'

After the show, Tom took Mickey home. The switchboard of the television studio was jammed with hundreds of callers wanting to find out more about Mickey. Many called to ask how they could get tickets to the National Swimming Championships, while others just called to congratulate him and wish him all the best. In the end, Mickey's first television interview was a success. That evening, Dolphin Boy Blue had made hundreds of fans!

CHAPTER THIRTEEN

'So what's wrong? What is it, Doc?' It was the morning of the big day – the Nationals. And Tom couldn't believe that Mickey was feeling sick. He'd heard Mickey sob and moan all night, but when he'd asked him what was wrong, Mickey had said, 'I don't know. I'm just feeling really weak.'

The doctor took Tom aside. 'Listen, Tom, there's nothing physically wrong with the boy. He hasn't got a temperature or any pains. It may be a bad case of nerves about today. And if it's not about today, then something else may be upsetting him.'

'Thanks, Doc.' As Tom showed him out, Mickey was left feeling terrible. He didn't want to let Tom and everyone else at Blue

Rock down. He wished he knew what was wrong with him.

'Mickey, I think it may be a good idea to take you to the pool – not to train, but just to have a splash around. Being in the water may make you feel better.' Mickey agreed.

Once at the pool, Tom could tell that Mickey was not his usual self. In the water, he looked sluggish and awkward and Tom called to him to hop out.

'Mate, what's wrong? Is it Dana?'

'I don't know what's wrong. It could be Dana, I haven't spoken to her for days and I'm really worried about her, Tom.'

'Get dressed,' said Tom, suddenly. 'We're going.'

'Going where?' asked Mickey.

'I'm taking you to Blue Rock, to see Dana.'

'But what about the race?'

'It's not until late afternoon, if we leave now, we'll be back in time. Just don't worry.' Tom knew that they would be cutting it very fine. It was a two and a half hour drive to Blue Rock, then they would have to get in the boat, find Dana, and then get back in time. But he felt it was worth the risk.

Before they left for Blue Rock, Tom called Terry and Judy and explained what was going on. Judy still planned to go to the city and wait for Tom and Mickey at the pool. Tom suggested that she try and stall the officials as long as she could if they were late getting back to town.

Tom put his foot down all the way, and just over two hours later they were heading into Blue Rock.

'We're here now. Everything's going to be all right,' Tom reassured Mickey. He drove along the beach front and down to the docks, where Terry was waiting with the boat. Jo and Madam Karma were there, too.

Mickey hopped out of the car and rushed over to his father, giving him a big hug.

'Don't worry, son, she'll be OK,' whispered Terry.

Madam Karma found herself standing next to Tom and, while all the greetings were going on, they smiled shyly at each other. They both felt that they had a lot more to say to each other somehow, but this was neither the time nor the place – they were here for Mickey.

'Here's my card. Call me when all this is over,' said Madam Karma, the more outgoing of the two.

Jo grinned at her and said, 'Grab your chances, eh?'

Madam Karma just winked.

Once out on the boat, Mickey, Terry, Tom, Madam Karma and Jo were all frantically searching the sea, hoping to spot Dana. But she was nowhere in sight. Terry headed the boat out to where they spotted her the last time – at the mouth of the ocean.

Jo tried chatting to Mickey to take his mind off his worries. 'You were great on TV. All the kids at school are talking about you.' But Mickey didn't respond. 'Hey, look, Mickey, whatever happens, I just want you to know I'm around, OK?'

Mickey looked up and stared at Jo for a moment. 'Thanks,' he said, looking distracted.

'Hey, son, put this on.' Terry threw Mickey a wetsuit. 'I don't want you jumping in with your clothes on this time. Besides, the water's freezing, you'll need it!'

Mickey put the wetsuit on but there was still no sign of Dana. Tom kept looking at his watch. Is history repeating itself? he thought. Like him, all those years ago? Was Mickey going to make it back in time to race?

'There she is!' Jo shouted. Dana was only a couple of hundred metres away, heading towards them.

Mickey jumped quickly into the icy water. Even with a wetsuit on, the grey ocean was still bitterly cold. He wouldn't be able to stay in for long without putting his health at risk. He dived down beneath the waves but he couldn't see much in front of him. The ocean was dark and deep. The further down he swam, the darker it got. The eerie silence of the enormous black depths below frightened Mickey a little. In his mind he called out to Dana – he knew she was near – her distant squeaks and clicks were coming closer.

Quite suddenly, Dana was there, staring at Mickey, nose-to-nose. Mickey was startled by her sudden appearance. He grabbed on to her tightly as they came up together for air. He was upset but overjoyed at seeing her again.

'I'm so sorry, Dana. I tried to talk to you, but I was always so tired. And I know something's wrong and—' Dana stopped him. She began to sing softly to him:

'Together we swim and all is right
Like the first time we met on that moonlit
night
I have seen you learn and watched you
grow
But now it is time for me to go.'

'Go? Go where?' Mickey clung to Dana, his teeth beginning to chatter with cold and alarm. He didn't have much time before he'd have to get back in the boat.

Mickey could see the sadness in Dana's eyes. 'I don't want you to go,' he said, finding it hard to hold back the tears.

'You must remember, no matter how long
To believe in yourself, and always be
strong
In your memory, I will always be
I will never forget, your love for me

Live by the dolphin, and do your best
My calling is done, now it's time for rest.'

'Rest? What do you mean, rest? Please, don't tell me you're going to die! You're not going to, are you, Dana? Dana, please! Don't go!'

But Dana didn't answer. With a strong flick of her tail she freed herself from Mickey's arms and dived swiftly down into the dark depths of the ocean. Taking a huge gulp of air, Mickey dived quickly after her. But it was no use – Dana was gone.

CHAPTER FOURTEEN

'Would Mickey Nolan of Blue Rock, please report to the marshalling area? This is your final call.' This was the third and last announcement for Mickey, but he and Tom still hadn't appeared. It looked as though Mickey was going to miss his race. Judy was desperately trying to persuade the officials to hold on for at least a few more minutes.

'Please, you have to wait! So many people will be disappointed and Mickey will be so upset!' she begged.

'Look, Miss,' said one of the officials. 'This is the Nationals. We can't change our schedule to suit one swimmer. Like most of this crowd here, I personally want Mickey to swim, but we can't hold on any longer.'

Reluctantly, Judy had to agree with the official. She was amazed to see that in the jam-packed stadium, a large section of the crowd were people who had come specially to see Mickey swim. For the first time, Mickey had his own cheering squad. There were Dolphin Boy Blue banners and Go Mickey! signs everywhere.

Many people were there because of Mickey's TV appearance and they were getting restless and frustrated that he hadn't arrived. Where was Dolphin Boy Blue? There were rumours and stories circulating around the stadium about where Mickey Nolan could be.

'I've heard he's not coming because his father's ill,' said one.

'Well, I've heard he's too nervous to swim,' said another.

'I've heard he's gone back to see the dolphin,' said someone else.

You could cut the atmosphere with a knife. The swimming centre was buzzing and excited. School bands were playing and one of the races had started; the level of noise at the pool was so loud, you couldn't hear yourself think.

One person who couldn't care less about Mickey's whereabouts was Paul Galloway. After his win at the State Championships, he was even more big-headed and loud-mouthed than before. He was the favourite, and he couldn't understand what all the fuss was about Mickey. I won before and I'll beat that jerk again, he thought. He's probably too much of a chicken, that's why he's not here! he thought.

Scattered around the pool among the crowd were television cameras. It was the first time that the National Schools' Swimming Championships had been televized, live, throughout the entire country. There was even a commentary box, with a couple of commentators rambling on to the viewers.

'Welcome back to the Nationals! If you've just joined us, then you've already missed some fantastic races. Coming up next, with just under five minutes to go, is the boys' thirteen-and-under fifty-metre freestyle. The favourite to win is Paul Galloway of City Grammar. But I like the look of the boy from Western College, and Mickey Nolan from Blue Rock High. Although it doesn't seem like he— '

Back in Blue Rock, the main street was like a ghost town. Every store owner had shut up shop to be back home in time to watch Mickey swim.

Terry and Jo sat together watching the live broadcast. 'It doesn't look as if they did get back in time,' said Terry, anxiously.

Madam Karma was watching, too, back in her store, and all the students and teachers at Blue Rock High were crammed into the school hall watching a big screen. Dominique and her friends had pushed their way to the front and she'd made up a story to her family and friends, telling them that she and Mickey had always been close, and that he was going to swim for her!

Back at the pool, the commentators were still talking. 'We've just heard that the boy they're calling Dolphin Boy Blue, Mickey Nolan from Blue Rock High – you may have read about him or seen him on *The Andy Ball Show* last week – isn't here, and it doesn't look as if he's going to swim. That's a shame because— Hold on, something's happening— '

All of a sudden, Mickey came running through the stadium, with Tom a few steps behind. They'd made it! There was a huge roar from the crowd as they cheered and applauded Mickey, who'd arrived just in time to sign on. Judy hugged Tom and they went quickly to find their seats.

Paul Galloway snarled and rolled his eyes up – once again, he was ready to try and put Mickey off as the boys were making their way to the starting blocks.

'Hey, nerd! What took you so long?' Mickey didn't even hear Paul, he was still thinking about Dana.

'So you're famous now – I suppose I should call you dolphin-head.' Paul laughed wickedly. 'See you still have those pretty little shorts! Hey, I hope you're listening to me, nerd, you're not going to win. I'm gonna be the national champion!'

Now they were standing behind the starting

blocks, ready to begin the race. The swimmers' names were being announced to the crowd, lane by lane.

'Lane four, from City Grammar, Paul Galloway!' There was a huge roar from his cheering squad.

The television viewers were getting the full commentary. 'Well, viewers, the atmosphere here is electric. This race will be terrific. For you at home who aren't too familiar with how the swimmers are placed in their lanes, let me explain quickly. The middle lanes are the faster lanes; the fastest qualifier for this final gets lane four. In this case, it's Paul Galloway from City Grammar. The second fastest qualifier gets lane three, the third, lane five, and so on. The slowest qualifier gets lane eight, which in this case is Mickey Nolan.

'But let me stress that this doesn't mean a thing. Only a second and a half separate the eight swimmers. Any one of them could win today! Now they're about to start!'

The cheers and screams in the stadium had died down. There was complete silence.

*

Back at Blue Rock High, the students were completely quiet, too. Judy grabbed on to Tom's hand, just like Jo was doing with Terry, and Madam Karma had her fingers crossed. Standing on the starting block, Mickey looked directly ahead of him. He could see the other end of the pool and his heart was pounding. His stomach felt as if it was twisted into a hundred knots.

'Swim like a dolphin, swim like a dolphin,' he repeated, over and over to himself. Although he was oblivious of everything around him, the television cameras had focused directly on Mickey.

Suddenly, and for no apparent reason, Mickey felt their presence and stared straight into one of the cameras. As he did so, he grabbed hold of the dolphin pendant around his neck, and mouthed the words, 'Hi, Jo.'

In Blue Rock, Jo jumped up hysterically.

'That's it! That's the sign! That's the sign! Did you see that, Mr Nolan?' Terry was more than a little confused by Jo's wild dance. 'I don't believe it! Mickey's about to swim the race of his life and he says "Hi, Jo". I LOVE

YOU, MICKEY!' shouted Jo at the TV. Terry grinned.

'Please, Jo, sit down. The race is about to start!'

'On your marks— ' BANG-BANG!

The gun had shot twice, signalling a false start. It was Mickey! A ripple of oohs and aahs from the crowd echoed around the stadium. One of the officials crossed over to Mickey and told him that if he did a false start again, he would be automatically disqualified.

Madam Karma gazed intently at her television screen. 'Focus, Mickey, focus!'

Jo and Terry urged him on. 'Come on, son, just concentrate, you'll be all right.'

So did Tom and Judy. 'Oh, Tom, I'm so nervous for him,' she said, clinging on to his arm in her anguish.

The boys were out of the water and back on their starting blocks again. As before, the crowd went silent.

'Take your marks— ' BANG! This time it was a clean start. As soon as the boys hit the water, the stadium erupted in a frenzy of deafening screams and cheers.

'Go, Paul!' 'Come on, Mickey!' 'Faster, City Grammar!' 'Go for it, Western College!' 'GO! GO! GO!'

All eight swimmers made a great start, so much so that, with half a lap to go, no-one could tell who was winning. It was extremely close.

Mickey thrashed his arms and kicked faster than he'd ever done before. 'I'm as fast as a dolphin. Swim like a dolphin!' he kept saying to himself. Every time he took a breath, he could hear the muffled screams of the crowd. It looked as if everything was happening in slow motion; the crowd was jumping up and down, their mouths wide open, cheering the swimmers on.

Back in Blue Rock, the whole town was out of their seats, shouting at their television sets.

At the High School, they were hysterical. 'Come on, Mickey! Come on!' they chanted.

Madam Karma was equally excited: 'You can do it, pet, just believe!'

Jo and Terry were jumping up and down. 'Go on, son! You can do it!'

Tom and Judy, like everyone else, were

standing on their seats now, totally caught up in the electric excitement of the race.

Even the commentators were losing their voices from shouting. 'It's gonna be close! Lane four and lane eight are slightly in front!'

With only fifteen metres to go, the race was between Paul and Mickey again!

In the water, Mickey could see the end of the pool. He wanted to breathe, but decided not to. He was in pain and every muscle in his body was straining to get to that wall. Suddenly, into his head came the clicks and squeaks of Dana. She was singing their song once again:

> 'Sing away those broken tears
> I am here for you
> Swim away unwanted fears
> No need of me for you
> I love you, Mickey. I'll always love you.'

Only metres from the end, Mickey still heard Dana's voice and then, out of the blue, he recognized an echo of a long-forgotten one – his mother's.

With one large swooping stroke, Mickey

thumped the wall! He looked up as he surfaced to see the results flash across the electronic board. 'Lane eight – first!' Mickey had won!

There was jubilation in the stadium and in Blue Rock! From that moment on, Mickey knew that Dana had gone and, with her, the last bond with his mother.

But he also knew that he could do it on his own now – with the help and love of his father and friends.

The sun was setting over the bay at Blue Rock and Dana, slowly and peacefully, swam out towards the horizon...

GOLDEN MOMENTS

☆

Felice flays record

Young Kyabram swimming star Felice Arena (pictured) shattered the Under 14 50m butterfly record in the Victorian All Junior Swimming Association Championships held at the State Centre in Melbourne last weekend.

Felice, a Kyabram High School student, broke the records in his heat and then went on to take the championship.

He clocked 29.82 seconds his heat win, bettering the old mark of 30.35.

Felice won his heat by five metres but had a tougher swim in the final to win by about 1½m in a time of 30.28 seconds.

Felice won the event in the Under 13 section last year.

FASALA THRILL FOR FELICE

Many young swimmers dream of racing against some of Australia's greats, such as Olympic silver medallist, Greg Fasala from the "mean machine".

Kyabram's Felice Arena has done just that.

Not only did Felice race against Fasala, but he also came third to him.

GOLD FOR FELICE

Kyabram swimmer Felice Arena brought home a gold medal as a result of the Shell All Junior Championships held at the state pool in Melbourne last weekend.

Competing in the 13 years section, Felice's successful swim was in the 50 metre butterfly.

Felice was also a finalist in the 50 metre freestyle being placed 4th. He also gained 7th place in the final of the 50 metre backstroke.

⊛ FACTFILE: FELICE ARENA

Age: Early twenties

Born: Victoria, in sunny Australia

Now lives: London, England

Talents: Endless! He was a state swimming champion; played basketball for his school; can act, dance and sing; enjoys writing and painting; and even speaks fluent Italian!

Big break: Playing the role of gorgeous Marco in *Neighbours*.

Other claims to fame: Guest presenter on *Disney TV*, and has appeared on *The Big Breakfast* and *Noel's House Party*.

Most daunting roles: Playing Jesus in *Godspell* and appearing naked on stage in *Hair*.

What he could have been: Your teacher! Felice is a trained schoolteacher.

What he wanted to be: An Olympic Gold Medallist

What he's going to be: Appearing in a town near you in *What a Feeling!* with Sonia and Irene Cara.

 Don't miss him.

A FINAL MESSAGE FROM FELICE...

As you may imagine, Australia's oceans are full of dolphins, but my first experience of swimming with a dolphin was off the coast of Israel. It was a lifetime dream come true. She even let me stroke her!

However, what is not so easily imagined is that dolphins can also be found in the UK. In fact, twenty-five species have been recorded in the North Sea and English Channel, but the numbers have depleted and they are under constant threat from pollution, entanglement in fishing nets, and reduction in fish stocks.

If you would like to know more about dolphins or whales, you can write to:

The Whale and Dolphin Conservation Society,
Alexander House,
James Street West,
Bath, Avon
BA1 SBT

Felice Arena